The Clue in the Old Stagecoach

"Have you found the clue?" Nancy asked excitedly

NANCY DREW MYSTERY STORIES

The Clue in the
Old Stagecoach

BY CAROLYN KEENE

GROSSET & DUNLAP
Publishers • New York

Contents

The Clue in the Old Stagecoach

CHAPTER I

The Mysterious Stagecoach

"Nancy, this is one of the steepest hillsides I've ever climbed down," said Bess Marvin. "I hope the mystery you're about to solve will be worth all this trouble."

The pretty, blond girl was with two companions who were carefully picking their way down a wooded slope. One was Nancy Drew, tall, slender, and attractive, with blue eyes, and hair with just a hint of titian. The other was Bess's cousin George Fayne, a boyish, slim girl, who was a sparkling brunette with a good sense of humor.

Nancy smiled. "I wonder what Mrs. Strook is going to ask me to do." At that moment Nancy was looking through a long clearing to the road below. Her eyes widened in amazement. "Girls, look!" she cried out.

Bess and George gazed downward just in time

to see four white horses pulling an old stagecoach. Evidently the horses were running away. There was no driver, but inside the stagecoach the girls could glimpse two swaying figures.

George clapped a hand to her forehead. "Am I dreaming or have I jumped back in time a hundred years?"

"I don't know what this means," Nancy replied, "but we must try to stop that runaway!" She darted down the hillside.

"But they'll be way ahead of us by the time we get there," Bess argued.

"We'll go at an angle and head them off!" Nancy retorted, changing course.

George soon caught up to Nancy. Bess was a little distance behind. The girls turned their ankles and lost their balance on the uneven, stony ground. They grabbed for tree trunks to steady themselves and finally reached the foot of the hill.

"There they are!" George exclaimed.

"The horses have stopped," Nancy added, as the two girls emerged onto a narrow country road.

A few seconds later Bess arrived. By this time Nancy and George were laughing merrily.

"What's so funny?" Bess asked, puzzled.

Her cousin pointed, and Nancy explained, "The horses are artificial. They're made of plaster of Paris, I guess. And they're attached to a wheeled platform."

Bess stared in astonishment. "But the stage-coach—what about that?"

"I'm sure it's authentic," Nancy replied.

Pulling open one of the side doors of the stage-coach, which was painted bright red with gold decorations, she said, "Those figures on the rear seat are plastic dummies and here on the floor are the rest of the group!"

One after the other she lifted out the driver and the messenger. Both men wore tight-fitting pants, high boots, gray wool jackets over white shirts, and flat, black, low-crowned hats with wide brims.

The women passengers were dressed in flower- and ribbon-trimmed bonnets, tight bodices, and toe-length bouffant skirts. The men dummies wore suits in light shades with knee-length, rather snug coats, and high-crowned hats.

Bess was laughing now too. "We won't have to go on to Mrs. Strook's," she said. "We have a mystery on our hands right here."

"We certainly have," George agreed. "What do you suggest we do about it?"

"It's my guess," Nancy said, "that somebody was towing this antique outfit, and it broke loose." She pointed to two link chains attached at each side of the front of the horses' platform.

"In that case," George spoke up, "the person will certainly be back."

Bess looked worried. "We don't know when,

though. I think we ought to guard the stagecoach until he arrives."

At that moment the girls saw a truck approaching from the opposite direction. As it came up to them, the handsome young driver stopped and leaned out the cab window.

"I got a good distance up the road before I realized my tow chain had broken," he said. "I'm glad nothing happened to the old outfit."

Bess smiled. "We thought we were seeing things as we came down through the woods from Camp Merriweather. We're vacationing there. Where is this stagecoach going?"

The truck driver introduced himself as John O'Brien, then said, "I guess you girls haven't heard about the deserted village of Bridgeford that's being restored."

"No, we haven't," Nancy replied.

John explained that about two miles away there had once been a thriving town where iron ore was brought from a nearby bog to be smelted. It had been abandoned a hundred years before, but now the county historical society, with the help of some people interested in reconstructing old villages, was fixing up the place.

"A woman named Mrs. Pauling, who lives outside of Francisville," John O'Brien went on, "bought this stagecoach and had it repaired and newly painted. It came from an abandoned farm.

The people who bought the place recently found it hidden on the property."

"The horses too?" George asked.

"No. Mrs. Pauling had them made. She's presenting the whole thing to the restoration at the time of the grand opening. You ought to come over and see what's being done."

"I'd like to," said Nancy.

By this time the trucker had stepped out of the cab and was inspecting the tow chains. One large piece was attached to his truck and he explained that the two lighter ones on the horses' platform had snapped off. After turning the truck around, he produced more links from a toolbox and repaired the tow.

Whistling, John O'Brien got behind the wheel of the truck, waved to the girls, and said, "Don't forget to come over to Bridgeford."

"We'll be there," Nancy called as he drove off. She looked at her wrist watch. "Girls, we're going to be dreadfully late for our appointment with Mrs. Strook. Let's hurry!"

Mrs. Strook, an elderly woman, lived in Francisville. Formerly a quiet place with a small population, it had suddenly mushroomed because of two housing developments which had sprung up not far apart at one end of the village. Less than half an hour's walk brought the three girls to the shaded side street where Mrs. Strook lived.

"What a charming place!" Bess remarked, as they reached a small, white, two-story colonial house surrounded by a white picket fence with a gate. Flowers, especially old-fashioned American varieties, grew in profusion in the front yard.

Mrs. Strook, a petite, smiling woman with snow-white hair pulled straight back and arranged in a knot at the nape of her neck, ushered the girls in with old-time courtesy.

"You have had a long, hot walk," Mrs. Strook said, as they cast admiring glances at the beautiful antique furniture, hooked rugs, and hand-woven linen draperies. "Won't you sit down while I bring some iced tea?"

Their charming hostess was gone only a few minutes, then returned with a tray and brimming glasses. As she and her guests sipped the delicious minted tea, Mrs. Strook looked intently at Nancy. "I probably shouldn't intrude on your vacation, but when I heard through the manager that you're staying at Merriweather and love to solve mysteries, I couldn't refrain from asking you to come over here. Let me tell you my story and then you can decide for yourself whether or not you want to help me."

Mrs. Strook said that the town of Francisville had been her family's home for many generations. At present the old-timers found it impossible to cope with the changed situation. The two hous-ing developments had brought many new families into the community. This had necessitated extensive water and sewage systems.

"Our town has issued bonds to borrow money for these," Mrs. Strook explained. "Now we find it impossible to issue any more for a much-needed educational program. We ought to have a large, new school. The old building cannot take care of all the children who have moved in."

As the woman paused, George spoke up. "Can't your town borrow money from the federal government?"

"A certain amount, my dear," Mrs. Strook answered. "And the town can add its share, of course. But what we need is a large sum to pay the balance. And that's where my mystery comes in."

The elderly woman's eyes twinkled. "I had a great-uncle named Abner Langstreet. He never married. Great-uncle Abner was born in Francisville and loved our little village. But back in 1853, in September to be exact, he disappeared, taking all his savings with him.

"None of his relatives or friends ever saw him alive again, but ten years later word came to my grandmother, his sister, that Great-uncle Abner had been found dead in a small farmhouse only a few miles from here. He had become a hermit, but evidently just before his death he decided to reveal a certain secret that he had been harboring since leaving Francisville.

"An unfinished letter to my grandmother was discovered and in it Abner Langstreet said that he was sorry he had run away and hoped it had caused the family no embarrassment. But he had not been able to face the bankruptcy he saw confronting him. The railroad which came here in 1852 had ruined his business. The tracks are gone now, but you can see the embankment here and there."

As Mrs. Strook paused again, Bess asked, "What was your great-uncle's business?"

"He was a stagecoach driver—owned his own coach and horses."

The three girls sat up very straight in their chairs. Twice, within an hour, they were hearing about an ancient stagecoach!

"You see," Mrs. Strook went on, "everyone began to use the railroad and there were no more passengers for my great-uncle. He was heartbroken and left Francisville in the old stagecoach without telling anyone. It was thought that he had gone out West to drive it or at least to sell it. You know, stagecoaches were used in the western part of our country long after they went out of vogue in the East.

"Lately," the elderly woman went on, "I have begun to think that Great-uncle Abner might not have taken his stagecoach so far away. If it was hidden around here, the old vehicle should be found and donated to the Bridgeford restoration."

"And you want me to find it?" Nancy asked.

"Yes, but not just for that reason. I have a more important motive—one that was written in the letter to my grandmother," Mrs. Strook replied quickly. "The letter said:

> *You will find a clue in the old stagecoach which may prove to be of great value to my beloved town of Francisville. I put it there because I wanted it to be found some day, but not for many years. I was afraid I might die suddenly, then no one would ever know. But now I shall tell you the secret. You will find the—*"

Mrs. Strook wiped away a tear which was trickling down one cheek. "The letter ended there," she said. "Apparently Mr. Langstreet was never able to write any more." She gazed at Nancy. "Do you think my story sounds too farfetched? I have been afraid of being laughed at if I go to the authorities with it. But I thought maybe you—"

Nancy had already risen from her chair. Now she sat down on the floor in front of the elderly woman and took both her hands in her own.

"I don't think your story is farfetched at all," she said. "I'd love to solve the mystery for you if I can. Now I'm going to tell you a strange coincidence. Bess and George and I saw an old stagecoach not far from here."

"What!" Mrs. Strook exclaimed.

When Nancy finished the story, Mrs. Strook stared in amazement. "You say this stagecoach was found hidden on a farm near here? Then it may very well have been my great-uncle's!"

"And contains the clue!" Bess cried out.

"Oh, I hope you're right!" Mrs. Strook said, her cheeks glowing and her eyes glistening with tears. "Could you find out for me?"

"Indeed we can," Nancy replied. "Bess and George and I will go back to the lodge and get my car. We'll drive to Bridgeford at once and examine the old stagecoach."

CHAPTER II

A Special Search

BEFORE leaving, Nancy asked Mrs. Strook if she had a photograph of Abner Langstreet's stage-coach.

"Yes, I have," she answered. "It's upstairs. I'll get it."

Nancy's mind was leaping ahead; she might solve the mystery that very day!

The young sleuth had already figured out the answers to several mysteries, some of them for her father, Carson Drew. He practiced law in River Heights where Nancy, Bess, and George lived. Among the cases on which Nancy had helped him were *The Secret in the Old Clock* and *The Golden Pavilion*, the latter in the Hawaiian Islands.

Presently George said in a low tone to the other two girls, "Suppose Mr. Langstreet went a bit zany in his seclusion and imagined the whole thing."

"Oh, George," Bess scolded, "you're so practical. Why don't you look at the romantic side of it? I'm sure the story is true. What do you think, Nancy?"

"I have a strong hunch there's something to it," the young sleuth answered.

"You see, George, you're outvoted," her cousin said. "Just for that, if you lose, you'll have to pay us a forfeit."

Nancy's eyes twinkled. "You certainly will, George. Bess, let's make it something good. I'll tell you what. George, if we win, you'll have to knit each of us a lovely sweater!"

George groaned. The other two girls knew she hated to knit. "Oh, please not that!" she begged.

Bess winked at Nancy. "Sweaters or nothing," she answered.

Before George could object any further, Mrs. Strook came down the stairs holding a faded photograph. It showed four proud-looking, coal-black horses hitched to an attractive stagecoach. Nancy asked if she might take the picture along to compare it with the stagecoach at Bridgeford.

"Yes, indeed, my dear," Mrs. Strook answered. "And I shall be eagerly awaiting your answer."

The girls said good-by and started for the front door. Nancy opened it and almost ran full tilt into a man and a woman who were standing on the other side. They were Mr. and Mrs. Ross Monteith, who were staying at Camp Merriweather.

Ross and Audrey were in their early thirties. They were not popular with the younger set who considered them too aggressive and overeager to be included where they were not welcome.

Ross was tall and slender, with dark hair and piercing black eyes. His manner of speaking was very affected. Audrey, blond and blue-eyed, was a braggart. She attempted by her speech and mannerisms to appear more sophisticated than she actually was.

"Why, Nancy Drew, fancy meeting you here!" said Ross. "Audrey and I were out for a hike. Isn't this place utterly charming—best-looking house in town. We're thirsty and we thought we'd step in for some water."

"Do you know the owner?" Nancy asked.

"No, but we hope to meet him or her."

Mrs. Strook, who had followed the girls to the door, stepped forward. She was frowning and it was evident that she was annoyed by the intrusion. "If you will take seats out in the garden, I will bring you some ice water," she said.

"Oh, I'll take it to them," Bess offered.

Ross and Audrey Monteith went to sit in chairs under a large shade tree. In a few minutes Bess carried out two tall glasses of ice water.

"Thanks," said Ross. "Are you girls going back to the lodge?"

"I really don't know," Bess replied and walked away.

In the house George whispered to Mrs. Strook, "I'm glad that you didn't invite the Monteiths in. They're staying at our camp and are very inquisitive people."

Mrs. Strook smiled knowingly. Then she said, "By the way, please don't tell my little secret about the stagecoach to anyone, will you?"

The three girls promised to keep the matter in strictest confidence, then they said good-by and hurried off. As they reached the hillside trail and began climbing toward the summit, George remarked, "I think Ross and Audrey deliberately followed us and I'm afraid they were eavesdropping near the open window."

"I agree," said Bess.

Nancy was inclined to think so too. "Anything they missed I'm sure they won't learn from Mrs. Strook!" she said with a grin.

After the arduous climb the three girls reached the extensive plateau on which Camp Merriweather stood. The main building was a large, rambling log cabin with pine-paneled interior walls. In front of it was an immense swimming pool with sun umbrellas and tables set around the edge. At once the three girls were besieged by a group of young people who invited them to go swimming.

"We can't just now," Nancy called. "Have a job to do."

"A mystery to solve?" asked one of the young

men, coming to her side. He was Rick Larrabee, tall, very blond, and an excellent dancer. Nancy had enjoyed having dates with him during her stay at camp.

"A detective never tells her secrets," she said, laughing. "But I promise we'll all join you later."

"I'll hold you to that," Rick replied.

Nancy, Bess, and George quickly showered and changed their clothes. Then they set off in Nancy's convertible for Bridgeford. The old town, situated about a mile from the main road, was a beehive of activity.

"Oh, this is simply wonderful!" Bess cried out in delight, gazing around at the quaint buildings, some of which had been restored.

"I like that covered bridge," George spoke up. "I suppose it led to what was the main road in olden days."

"This rushing stream was used to turn the water wheel in that old mill," Nancy remarked. Some distance up the stream stood the miller's vine-covered cottage. The great wheel and the grinder were in a wing of the house.

The girls walked around for a while, inspecting the ancient bakery which as yet held no food; the blacksmith's shop with its fire pit, anvil, and smoke-stained walls; and finally what a workman told them had been the "artillery house."

"What does that mean?" Bess asked.

The man explained that it had once contained

firearms—rifles, pistols, cannon, together with bullets, gunpowder, and other weapons for helping ward off unexpected attacks from enemies."

"You mean like Indians?" Bess inquired. The workman nodded.

As the girls walked off, Nancy said, "Perhaps we've done enough sight-seeing and should find the old stagecoach." She was about to ask another workman where it was when the girls saw John O'Brien coming toward them.

He smiled broadly. "I thought I saw you here," he said. "Let me show you around."

Nancy thanked him but said, "We're eager to look at the stagecoach."

John O'Brien told the visitors to follow him, and led the way to an old barn which had not yet been repaired. As he opened the creaking door, the man said, "There she is. I detached the horses. They're in another barn."

"May we inspect the stagecoach?" Nancy asked.

"Sure. Go ahead. But don't damage anything."

John O'Brien said he had an errand to do in another part of the village. When he finished he would be back. The young man strode off and instantly the girls began to investigate the ancient vehicle.

Nancy took the photograph of old Mr. Langstreet's stagecoach from her purse to compare it with this coach. She stood off at a short distance and surveyed the one in the barn, then stared at the picture. The design and size were identical!

A pleased smile came over her face. "Girls, it looks as if this might have been Great-uncle Abner's stagecoach!"

"Super!" said George. "Now let's find that clue!"

After a short conference, it was decided that George would search the driver's seat and the box under it. Nancy would examine the interior, while Bess investigated the "boot" at the rear. This was a great triangular leather sack attached to the back of the stagecoach to hold baggage.

There was complete silence for many minutes as the girls worked. George went over every inch of the driver's seat, removing the cushion and looking thoroughly in the leather-lined box beneath. She found nothing.

Nancy had no better luck inside. She had turned up and thoroughly examined under and around the cushions on the front and rear seats, and the one in the center. She had felt the padded walls and looked for any opening. Then she had dropped to her hands and knees for an examination of the floor. Finally she came to the conclusion that no clue was going to be found easily.

Just then Bess gave a loud squeal. George and Nancy jumped to the ground and ran to her side.

"Have you found the clue?" Nancy asked excitedly.

Bess had unbuckled the cover of the "boot"

and inside had found a newspaper dated 1860. Quickly she laid it on the ground and carefully turned the pages, skimming through the various items and advertisements which might yield the clue for which they were hunting.

Finding nothing, she turned back to the first page and this time all the girls went over each article minutely. Still they found nothing to help them.

"Oh dear!" said Bess. "I thought sure I had solved the mystery!"

The newspaper was put back into the "boot" and the fastenings closed.

"If the clue is in this stagecoach, it's well concealed," Nancy remarked. "I wonder if we could possibly look inside the cushions and other hiding places."

At that moment John O'Brien returned. He seemed to be excited. "Come on with me, quick!" he exclaimed. "They're going to put the water wheel into operation. It hasn't turned in a hundred years!"

The three girls hurried along beside him up the towpath which led to the miller's home. There were a few sight-seers present, but the bulk of the audience was comprised of people working on the restoration.

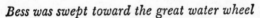

Bess was swept toward the great water wheel

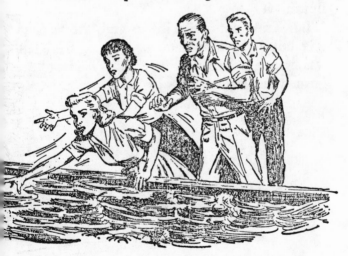

They crowded into the small cellar room which contained part of the sluiceway leading to the big wheel. The girls became separated from John O'Brien and were pushed against one of the wooden sides of the sluiceway.

"Everyone set?" called a man standing not far from Nancy. He had one hand on a great wooden lever which could divert the water to or from the great wheel.

"Guess we are!" came a reply.

The man pushed the lever with all his might. Instantly tumbling, gushing water rushed into the sluiceway, headed for the wheel's blades. At the same instant the crowd surged forward to watch.

An overeager man stumbled into Bess and knocked her off balance. Unable to steady herself, the astonished girl tumbled headlong into the sluiceway!

Bess cried out and tried to grab the wooden side, but the rushing water was too powerful. She was swept along toward the turning blades of the great water wheel!

CHAPTER III

An Ominous Warning

When Nancy and George realized what had happened to Bess, the two girls made a wild leap forward and grabbed for her in the sluiceway. Water spurted in all directions over the stunned onlookers, as Nancy and George managed to pull their chum to safety.

"You all right, young lady?" cried out the man who had turned the lever.

"Y-yes," Bess sputtered.

She was a bedraggled sight, with her hair and clothes hanging limp! "Please, let's go home," she said plaintively.

"Right away," Nancy replied.

The worker who had jostled Bess off balance apologized profusely, and asked if there was anything he could do.

The forlorn girl shook her head. "No, thanks."

The man in charge of the mill now ordered

everyone out of the place. Coming over to the girls, he said, "I'm mighty sorry this happened. Thank goodness you weren't hurt."

The three friends left hurriedly and headed at once for Nancy's car. John O'Brien, who only a moment ago had realized that Bess was the victim of the accident, caught up to the girls and offered to do whatever he could.

"I'll be all right," Bess assured him.

Nancy said that she had a raincoat in the back of the car which Bess could put on during the drive back to Camp Merriweather.

"Outside of the little accident, we really had a wonderful time here," Nancy told John O'Brien. "Thank you for suggesting we come."

The trucker saluted and went off to his job. The girls were soon back at the lodge.

"I'll pull into an inconspicuous spot in the parking yard," Nancy told Bess. "Then we can go up the back stairway and nobody will question you."

"Thanks," said Bess. "I suppose you mean the Monteiths."

Unfortunately, the three girls had no sooner stepped from the convertible than they were confronted by Ross and Audrey who appeared like apparitions out of the bushes that surrounded the parking area.

"Why, Bess Marvin!" Audrey Monteith cried out. "Whatever have you been doing to yourself?"

"I had a little swim," Bess returned tersely.

As if disbelieving Bess's words, Audrey pulled aside the raincoat the girl was wearing. Seeing the soggy clothing beneath, she remarked, "But not a swim you intended to take."

Bess offered no further explanation. Nancy and George did not say a word as the three walked up a path toward the rear of the lodge. Audrey and Ross followed close behind.

"Mrs. Strook is a delightful old lady, isn't she?" Ross queried.

"Yes, she is," Nancy answered.

"Have you known her a long time?" Ross prodded.

"Long enough to feel that I know her rather well."

"So you won't talk?" Audrey remarked. "Nancy, you don't have to be so tight with your information. Tell us, why did you and Bess and George go to see Mrs. Strook?"

Nancy and her friends were annoyed, but resolved not to lose their tempers. George, however, could not resist a remark. "Like you and your husband, we had a cool drink there—only ours was iced tea."

The Monteiths looked at each other as if to say, "We're not going to find out anything now," and hurried down a side path.

Bess fumed, "Nancy, first thing you know those

two horrible creatures will be taking the mystery right out of your hands and trying to solve it themselves!"

Nancy was silent for a few seconds, then she set her jaw firmly. "Let them try it!" she said.

When the girls reached their rooms, Nancy suggested that they put on bathing suits and go for a real swim. Bess grinned. "My second today. And anyway, we promised Rick and the others we'd join them later."

For the next few hours the three girls thoroughly enjoyed themselves. There was no mention of the mystery until they were preparing for bed. Then George asked Nancy how she planned to continue searching for the clue in the old stagecoach.

"I'm going to ask Mrs. Strook's permission to tell part of her secret to Mrs. Pauling, the woman who owns the stagecoach. Maybe she'll let me make a more thorough search."

"That sounds like a good idea," Bess remarked. "When do you plan on going?"

"Monday morning."

Bess and George said they would have to be counted out as they had promised to play in a tennis match at that time.

"I'm sorry," said Nancy.

Next day, Sunday, the girls went to church in town. Later Nancy phoned Mrs. Strook's home and gave her the latest news.

"Do you think there's a good possibility that coach was Great-uncle Abner's?" the elderly woman asked eagerly.

"Yes," Nancy answered. "It certainly looks a lot like the picture. I thought perhaps Mrs. Pauling might let us investigate a little deeper. Do you know her?"

"Not personally," Mrs. Strook answered, "but I understand she's a fine woman and is very civic-minded. I believe she would keep my secret and at least tell us anything she may know. Yes, Nancy, go ahead and talk with her."

Directly after breakfast on Monday, Nancy drove to Mrs. Pauling's home. It was a large house built at the top of a knoll and reached by a winding driveway. In front of the house was a wooded area, screening the residence from the highway. Nancy could see barns and other buildings to the rear as she drove up and parked.

At the same instant she heard yelping dogs approaching, and within seconds she was surrounded by a pack of hunting hounds.

Nancy smiled. "They're cute—and harmless."

She was about to pick up her purse and get out of the car when from around the corner of the house bounded two very large police dogs. They began to bark noisily and instantly the hunting hounds slunk away.

The police dogs took up stations on either side of Nancy's convertible and from their ferocious expressions and unfriendly barks she knew that they would not allow her to alight from the car.

"This is a fine mess," Nancy told herself. "Now what am I going to do?"

As if in answer to her question, the front door opened. A woman of about sixty, wearing attractive sports clothes, hurried toward Nancy. "Rex, be quiet!" she commanded. "Brutus! That will do for now!"

There was instant obedience. Together the dogs trotted off around the side of the house.

"I'm sorry about such a reception," the woman said. "The dogs are having their morning run." She smiled engagingly. "You see, I am well protected."

Nancy laughed as she stepped from the car. "They were certainly on the job. I'm Nancy Drew from River Heights. I'm staying at Camp Merriweather. Are you Mrs. Pauling?"

"Yes."

"I'd like to talk to you a few moments if I may," Nancy said.

Mrs. Pauling's face broke into a broad smile. "You may talk, but don't try to sell me anything," she warned. Before Nancy could assure her that this was not her intention, the woman inquired, "Are you by any chance Carson Drew's daughter?"

"Why, yes, I am."

"Then you are most welcome here," said Mrs. Pauling. "Your distinguished father took care of a

case for my late husband and did a very fine job.
Mr. Pauling praised him many times for the
work."

"Dad's wonderful," Nancy said, as Mrs. Pauling
led the way into the house, then through a long,
wide hall and out a rear door to a beautiful patio
garden. "I'm up here on vacation and happened to
stumble on a mystery. It may concern the old
stagecoach you donated to Bridgeford. May I tell
you about it?"

"Please do," Mrs. Pauling said, as she indicated
comfortable chaise lounges and chairs. "Let's sit
down here." She stretched out on one of the
lounges while her caller chose a bamboo chair.

Nancy told about Mrs. Strook and her great-
uncle, Abner Langstreet. By the time she had
finished her story, Mrs. Pauling was leaning forward, listening intently.

"I'm certainly going to help all I can," she remarked. "If the men who worked on the old
stagecoach found anything in it, they failed to
tell me. But I'll phone the carpenter and the
painter at once and find out what they know."

Mrs. Pauling arose and walked to the ground-
level porch to use a wall telephone. As Nancy
waited, she picked up a local newspaper. There
were large headlines telling the sad plight of the
Francisville school children.

"Poor kids! If I could only find that clue,"
Nancy thought, "it might help the situation!"

When Mrs. Pauling returned, she said that the carpenter had not come across anything unusual while restoring the old stagecoach. But he admitted that he had not taken the vehicle completely apart. Something might be hidden, he thought, deep inside the cushions, behind the upholstered sides, or even between the leather lining and the wood of the compartment beneath the driver's feet. The painter could offer no help either.

Mrs. Pauling sat lost in thought for several seconds. Then she said, "Tomorrow morning I'll have John O'Brien bring the stagecoach back here. I'll ask the carpenter to come over. You and he can take the old stagecoach entirely apart if necessary to find this clue that is going to mean so much to the town of Francisville."

"Oh, that's wonderful!" cried Nancy, who felt like hugging the woman. "And may I bring along my friends who are vacationing with me?"

"By all means," Mrs. Pauling said graciously.

Nancy, eager to tell Mrs. Strook and Bess and George the good news, said good-by to Mrs. Pauling, hurried through the hall, and out the front door toward her car. As she neared the convertible, a tall, muscular man in work clothes strode from among the trees in front of the house. He was about fifty years of age and had a very sour expression.

"Are you Nancy Drew?" he asked, stepping directly toward her.

"Yes."

Suddenly the stranger began to wave a finger in Nancy's face. "I'm here to tell you," he cried out, "that I don't want all these city folks movin' in and ruinin' our countryside! Water pipes, electric lights, and now a new school that's goin' to cost a mint o' money to us taxpayers! I won't have it, I tell you!"

As the irate man paused for breath, Nancy, who had stepped back in dismay, said in defense, "I have nothing to do with all those things!"

"Yes you do!" the stranger shouted at the top of his voice. "You're part o' this whole deal! Now you keep your nose out o' our community affairs!"

He glared belligerently at Nancy. "If you don't," he warned, "you're goin' to get hurt!"

CHAPTER IV

Hard-fought Games

Too amazed to reply again, Nancy stared at the truculent stranger. As he burst into a second tirade, the two police dogs suddenly raced around the corner of the house and growled.

"Good boys!" Nancy cried out.

The intruder did not wait to find out whether the dogs were friendly or not. Turning on his heel, he ran with long strides and disappeared among the trees. The dogs raced after him, giving deep-throated barks.

Nancy waited. Within three minutes the dogs were back. Turning to step into her car, she saw Mrs. Pauling in the doorway. The thought occurred to Nancy that perhaps the woman might know the intruder. She asked her.

"No, I never saw him before," Mrs. Pauling replied. "What a dreadful creature! I arrived too late to hear all he was saying to you. At the end, though, it sounded like a threat."

Nancy admitted that it was. "I think I'll hurry down to the main road and see if I can find out who he is. He's probably running off in a car. I'll follow him."

The young sleuth jumped into her convertible and sped off. But when she reached the main road, there was no car in sight and no sign of the strange man.

"If he lives around here," Nancy told herself, "shopkeepers in town probably know him. I'll go into Francisville and make some inquiries."

As she drove along the tree-shaded main street, Nancy noted that all the buildings were old-fashioned, with the exception of a new large, brightly lighted supermarket. Seeing a quaint-looking drugstore, Nancy decided that the proprietor might be a good person to interview. The drugstore owner, a short, plump, jolly person, smiled at Nancy and asked what she would like.

"First some information," she said, returning the smile. "Then a few cosmetics."

She described the intruder at the Pauling estate, and without revealing the warning he had given her, told of his dislike for newcomers in the area. "Have you any idea who he might be?"

The druggist, Mr. Benfield, did not hesitate in his answer. "That sounds exactly like Judd Hillary. He's a bachelor and dislikes children. Furthermore, he has no use for city people and especially the ones who have moved into this community recently. He declares they're causing too many changes in our quiet little village."

"Would you call him a dangerous individual?" Nancy asked, chuckling.

"Oh, no, I'd just say queer—very queer."

Despite this reassurance, Nancy still felt a little worried. She could not forget Judd Hillary's glare of hate or his angry warning. She asked Mr. Benfield if there were many people in the community who felt the same as Mr. Hillary did.

"There are some. He's sort of a self-appointed chairman of the group. All of them complain about the raising of our taxes and the fact that the town will be bankrupt if we try to build a new school. It is true that we cannot afford the school, yet we badly need one. To accommodate all the children this fall it will be necessary to run classes from eight in the morning until six at night, and frankly I don't know how long our teachers are going to be able to stand this. And our money will certainly run out by spring."

"That's a shame," said Nancy and added with a smile, "I suppose your only solution is to have some good fairy leave a lot of money here."

"That's about the size of it," Mr. Benfield agreed.

To herself Nancy said, "Oh, I hope I can be the one to bring that windfall to Francisville!"

She bought a new compact, two tiny bottles of perfume for Bess and George, and some paper handkerchiefs. Then, thanking the druggist for his information, she left the shop.

Nancy drove directly to Camp Merriweather. When she reached her room, the young sleuth noticed that Bess and George were seated glumly in the adjoining bedroom. Quickly she went in and asked, "What's wrong?"

Bess heaved a tremendous sigh and George said, her words clipped and showing deep annoyance, "The sports director had drawings this morning for the tennis tournament. Bess and I decided to go into the doubles. We picked two names out of the grab bag. One guess."

"Not Ross and Audrey Monteith!" Nancy exclaimed.

"Nobody else," George replied. "Can you imagine such luck!"

"I'm so mad I don't even want to talk about it," Bess spoke up. "Nancy, tell us what you found out."

She and George listened attentively to the whole story. When Nancy reached the part about Judd Hillary's warning, both girls frowned.

"Oh, Nancy, maybe you'd better give up this mystery," Bess said fearfully. "At first it was fun. Now it sounds positively sinister."

"Mr. Benfield, the druggist in Francisville, thinks Judd Hillary is just queer, not dangerous.

I see no reason why he and I should ever meet again."

"Why, Nancy," said George admonishingly, "don't you realize that Judd Hillary somehow found out about your interest in helping the town of Francisville and followed you to Mrs. Pauling's?"

Nancy looked startled. "George, believe it or not, I didn't think of that. And you're absolutely right. Well, I promise you both I'll watch my step. If I forget, you two just reach out and grab me."

She went on to say that the following morning she and the cousins ought to be on hand to see the old stagecoach dissected. "If we find the clue, then we shan't have to worry any more about Judd Hillary, anyway."

The three girls had an early lunch, then a little later Nancy went to play tennis with Rick Larrabee, who had pulled her name out of the grab bag, he said. She looked at him, her eyes twinkling merrily; she had not put her own name in! Realizing Nancy had guessed the truth, Rick told her that he had not entered the tournament either.

"Just for that little joke I'll beat you!" Nancy said. "Then later we'll watch the doubles match between Bess and George and the Monteiths."

Nancy and Rick were pretty evenly matched. He won the first game. She took the second and third, he the next two. Points were hard fought, and every game went to deuce until the score was six all. Then Nancy crawled ahead and finally won eight to six.

"Congrats!" Rick said, coming to the net and shaking hands with her.

The doubles match between Bess and George and the Monteiths was just about to start. A good-sized crowd had gathered to watch it, knowing that all the players were excellent. There were cheers and groans from the side lines as the match progressed. Few people at the lodge liked the Monteiths and most of the onlookers were secretly hoping that they would be badly trounced.

But Ross and Audrey were skillful players. Game after game went forty all. George and Bess found themselves using every type of strategy they knew to win. Each side took a set and the third started as a real battle. Then Ross and Audrey began to tighten up. This proved to be their undoing. Bess and George won the set by a score of six to two!

The hand clapping was loud. The special friends whom the girls had made at Camp Merriweather rushed up to hug or congratulate the winners. Ross and Audrey Monteiths' faces were flushed and angry. They shook hands listlessly with the winners. Finding they were receiving no attention, the two finally left the court.

As Nancy, Bess, and George walked back together toward the lodge, Nancy said, "I'm terribly thrilled about the outcome and I wouldn't want you to miss the rest of the tournament for anything. But this may mean that you won't be able to help me solve the mystery."

George looked at her chum accusingly. "Why, Nancy Drew, do you think we'd walk out on you? The athletic director who is running this tournament will certainly understand and let us play when you don't need us. If he won't—why, we'll default if necessary!"

Nancy was thrilled by her friends' loyalty and said she hoped the schedules could be arranged so the girls could go on to win the tournament.

"You asked us to be with you tomorrow morning," George said. "And I want to be there myself when that old stagecoach is taken apart. You girls go ahead upstairs. I'm going to try to set up things. See you in a few minutes."

When she arrived upstairs, George told them, "Everything's fine with the committee. Bess and I will play again tomorrow afternoon."

The three girls started off early the next morning in Nancy's convertible. Instead of going directly to Mrs. Pauling's home, Nancy decided to take a narrow lane leading to the road on which John O'Brien probably would be towing the old stagecoach, and join him. Reaching it, they waited a little while for the trucker to come along. When he did not arrive, Bess suggested that probably he had been ahead of them.

"No doubt you're right," said Nancy. "We'd better go on."

When they reached the estate, they found Mrs. Pauling standing in front of the house. Nancy introduced her friends, then asked if the stagecoach had arrived.

"Not yet," Mrs. Pauling answered. "And I can't understand it. John O'Brien is usually very prompt. He's already an hour late."

She took her callers out to the garden patio and they sat down on the porch to chat. Half an hour went by and still the trucker did not come.

Mrs. Pauling, nervous about the delay, called the office of the Bridgeford restoration project and learned that John O'Brien had left the place hours before with the old stagecoach.

"Something has happened!" Bess said nervously when she heard the report.

Just then the telephone rang and Mrs. Pauling answered it. The girls could plainly hear a man's deep voice at the other end of the wire.

"Mrs. Pauling, this is John O'Brien. I—I have bad news for you. The old stagecoach has been hijacked!"

CHAPTER V

Three Sleuths

"HIJACKED!" Nancy murmured in disbelief.

Mrs. Pauling held the telephone receiver partly away from her ear, so that Nancy and her friends could hear the rest of what John O'Brien was reporting.

"I was towing the old stagecoach along a deserted road," he said, "when two masked men jumped out from among some trees and boarded the truck. They shut off the motor and dragged me to the ground. They bound and gagged me, and left me in the woods. Then the two of them unfastened the tow chain and went off with the stagecoach."

"How terrible!" Bess said.

"After they'd gone around a bend," the trucker went on, "I heard a motor start up, so I guess the men went off in either a car or a truck and took the old stagecoach with them.

"After a while I managed to get free and drove along the road looking for them, but they were gone. I stopped at the first farmhouse I came to— it's called Brookside. That's where I am now. Mrs. Pauling, I'm mighty sorry about the whole thing. What do you want me to do?"

"This is preposterous!" Mrs. Pauling exclaimed. "It wasn't your fault of course, John. Hold the phone a moment and I'll let you know what to do."

Mrs. Pauling put her hand over the mouthpiece and consulted the girls. She said that she did not know what to tell John, but that she supposed someone should notify the police at once.

"Yes," Nancy replied. "Why don't you tell him to do that and please ask him to wait where he is. I'd like to dash over there and make a search of the area for clues."

Mrs. Pauling nodded and requested the trucker to do this. Then she put the phone back into its cradle and gave a great sigh. By this time Nancy, Bess, and George, eager to be off, were ready to say good-by.

When they reached the Brookside farmhouse where John O'Brien was waiting, they found two state policemen already talking to him. The trucker introduced the girls, and told of their interest in the old stagecoach.

John O'Brien then went on with his story. "Both the men who grabbed me were tall fellows. One had blond hair, the other was dark. They didn't say a word, so I wouldn't recognize their voices."

"Did you notice anything else that would identify them?" asked Officer Gavin.

"Yes," John replied. "The dark-haired fellow had a slantwise scar across his left wrist. And the blond man, I'd say, is either a sailor now or has been one. He tied me with nautical knots."

"You sure were lucky to get yourself untied," remarked Officer Starr. "We'll radio in the full report right away and then start a search for those two hijackers."

While the state trooper was calling from his car, John O'Brien told the other officer that Nancy was an amateur detective. Gavin smiled and asked if she had any theory regarding the theft of the old stagecoach.

On her guard, Nancy smiled and countered with, "I understand there are a good many people in this area who are opposed to newcomers who are making changes and causing higher taxes. If this is true in Francisville, might it also be true regarding Bridgeford?"

Officer Gavin looked at Nancy searchingly. Then his eyes twinkled. "Is that a genuine guess on your part, Miss Drew, or are you keeping your real theory to yourself?"

Nancy's only answer was a laugh. When State

Policeman Starr finished his report, he suggested that he and Gavin start their search.

"Do you mind if we follow you?" Nancy asked.

"Not at all," Gavin answered. "But I suggest that you stay a fair distance behind us in case we run into any trouble."

"I understand," Nancy replied. She climbed in behind the wheel of her convertible as Bess and George slid in from the other side.

John O'Brien went back as far as the spot where he had been attacked. Then the officers excused him and he headed for Bridgeford.

The wheel tracks of the old stagecoach were visible only as far as the place where John O'Brien had heard the motor start up. Here the troopers found crosswise marks in the dirt. Officer Gavin said they indicated that planks had been set up from the road to the rear of a truck. Apparently the stagecoach had been pushed up this runway onto the larger vehicle and taken away.

The tire marks of the truck were easily traced to a hard-surface road some distance ahead. Here they turned to the right, then they mingled with the tracks of other trucks and cars.

Presently Officer Starr, who was driving the policemen's car, signaled that he was going to stop. Nancy pulled up behind him at the side of the road. He came back to speak to her.

"We figure the old stagecoach was probably

carried in a closed truck or van, but if it was an open vehicle, maybe someone can give us a clue. A quarter of a mile down the road there's a new development. We're going to inquire at each house along the road for a mile to find out if anyone noticed the old stagecoach. If you girls would like to help, suppose you ask at the houses on the right side. Officer Gavin and I will take the left."

Nancy was pleased to have the assignment and quickly accepted it. When they reached the settlement, she stopped in front of the second house on the right. George ran up to inquire at the first home, Bess to the third, while Nancy took the one in the center. None of the occupants answered their doorbells.

The policemen had no better luck across the street, so the two groups of inquirers moved on down the road. The same procedure followed. This time two of the residents were at home but neither of them had seen an open truck with an old stagecoach on it.

"Not a single clue," Officer Gavin said in disgust.

After the mile had been covered, each group reported failure to learn anything. The policemen thanked the girls and said they would take care of further questioning themselves.

"We'll be in touch with Mrs. Pauling to hear what you find out," Nancy told them.

Turning her car around, the young sleuth started back in the direction from which they had come. George demanded an explanation.

"I'm positive," said Nancy, "that those hijackers never came this far. It would be risky carrying the stagecoach for long on a public highway. I want to follow a hunch of mine; that is, the two hijackers went off this main road, taking the stagecoach with them. They may even have unloaded it and dragged it into the woods."

George was inclined to agree with Nancy and added, "Which side road are you going to pick, Nancy?"

"The first one those hijackers came to after they turned into the main road."

When Nancy reached the woods road from which they had emerged a little earlier, she once more turned the car around, then drove very slowly. The three girls watched intently for a little-used side road.

They had gone scarcely a thousand feet when Bess called out that she could see a trail through a wooded area. "It's probably a bridle path."

Nancy had already stopped. Bess and George quickly stepped from the car and hurried into the woods.

Within a few seconds George called back, "I think this is the road all right. Here are wheel tracks and footprints!"

Nancy locked the car, pocketed the key, and

hurried after the cousins. The three excited sleuths almost ran along the bridle trail in their eagerness to find the old stagecoach.

Suddenly Bess stopped short. "We've gone far enough to prove our point," she declared. "I think we should go back and tell the state police. I certainly don't want to meet those hijackers!"

"I can't say that I do myself," Nancy replied. "On the other hand, we're only guessing that these wheel tracks belong to the old stagecoach. I think we should have more proof. Those hijackers may have taken the old stagecoach so they can hack it apart and find the clue. I'm convinced that Mr. Langstreet's secret has leaked out somehow. If we can possibly keep the antique vehicle from being destroyed, I'd certainly like to do it."

"I would too," said George. "Come on!"

Bess followed reluctantly. Less than a quarter of a mile ahead, the girls found themselves at the edge of a treeless cliff. Here the bridle trail veered off down the wooded slope. The girls paused and looked toward the foot of the cliff.

"There it is!" George cried exultantly.

Below them was the stolen stagecoach, intact! It was lying on one side.

"It isn't smashed, thank goodness," said George. "All those hijackers wanted to do was to get rid of it. But why?"

Nancy did not try to answer the question. She was not sure that she agreed with George. Bess again showed fear and insisted that the three girls leave and report to the police.

"Let's split up," Nancy suggested. "Bess, you take my car key and go back for officers Gavin and Starr. If you can't find them, get two others. George and I will go down this hillside and see what we can find out about the stagecoach." She handed the key to Bess.

"I don't like this arrangement," Bess said, "but I'll do it. And *please* be careful!"

"We'll stay among the trees alongside the bridle trail just to make you happy," George promised her cousin.

Bess went off, running at top speed. Nancy and George carefully descended the wooded hillside. On the way they neither saw nor heard anyone.

"I'd certainly like to get a close look at the old stagecoach," George whispered. "Do you think we dare?"

Nancy suggested that they wait a few minutes. Then, if they saw no sign of anyone, they would go into the open and find out what they could about the overturned vehicle. Ten minutes went by. Complete silence. Nancy signaled to George that they would proceed.

Just as the two girls walked up to the old stage-coach, a man's deep voice commanded harshly, "Stand where you are!"

CHAPTER VI

Police Assistance

THEIR hearts pounding, Nancy and George stood stock-still. Though both had been startled by the command from the unseen speaker, the girls tried not to show any fear.

"Who are you?" Nancy asked her hidden opponent. The man did not reply to her question. Instead, he ordered the girls to retrace their steps.

"Why?" Nancy countered, trying to stall for time until Bess could bring the police to the spot.

"Do as I say!" the stranger growled.

By this time Nancy and George had concluded that the man did not intend to reveal his whereabouts and harm them. Regaining their courage, the girls decided to stay as long as possible.

"We saw this old stagecoach from the top of the cliff," George spoke up. "We'd like to look at it."

"You leave the old thing alone!" the stranger directed.

"We're not going to harm it," Nancy argued. "Does it belong to you?"

All this time she had been listening intently, trying to find out where the speaker was located. As he called back, she decided the man was hiding in a huge maple tree not far away. She concentrated on the spot.

"That's none of your business," the stranger returned. "Now get out of here!"

Nancy detected a slight movement among the leaves on one of the stout limbs. In a shaft of sunlight she saw a man's hand and forearm. There was a slantwise scar across the wrist!

"One of the hijackers!" Nancy thought. "His blond cohort is probably with him. I guess George and I had better leave and go to meet the police."

Aloud she said, "Sorry to have bothered you. We'll go now."

George was surprised, but did not question Nancy's decision. Together the two girls scrambled up the hillside among the trees. When they were out of earshot of the man, Nancy quickly told George what she had seen.

"Hypers!" George exclaimed, using her favorite expression. "We found the hijackers! I hope they won't leave before we can have them arrested!"

The thought spurred the girls on and soon they reached the top of the cliff. They ran full speed along the bridle path toward the main road. Half-way there they met Bess and officers Gavin and Starr racing down the road. Quickly Nancy told her story and the whole group rushed back, so that the troopers might capture the hijackers.

As they neared the cliff, Officer Starr said he thought it best if the girls did not go down the bridle path, since the men below might expect a second visit from that direction and be warned away. "We'll take the other side right through the forest," he said. "And you girls, please keep in the rear." He turned to Nancy. "Would you act as lookout? Stay near the trees at the edge of the ravine. If you see anything unusual, notify us by rolling a stone in our direction."

Nancy nodded and went to the left of the group. Halfway down the slope, she suddenly spotted the two hijackers coming from hiding. One carried a hatchet, the other a large saw. Instantly they began to hack at the old stagecoach!

Seeing this, Nancy quickly sent a small stone hurtling down toward the policemen and beckoned them to come forward. "The hijackers!" she told them when they arrived, and pointed.

The officers gave one look, then ran pell-mell down the hillside. The three girls joined the chase. They had almost reached the foot of the slope when suddenly from somewhere in the woods came an unusual whistle. When the two hi-

"The hijackers!" Nancy warned

jackers heard it, they took to their heels and disappeared among the trees in the opposite direction.

Instantly the officers gave chase. Nancy did not follow. Instead, she said to her friends, "Let's try to find that whistler. He must be a pal of the hijackers."

They could hear crashing in the undergrowth not far from them, and took off in pursuit. But presently the sounds stopped and they could see no one. Finally the girls gave up.

"We'd better return and guard the old stagecoach," Nancy said. The others nodded.

When they got back, Nancy remarked, "One thing has been proved. There are at least three people involved in the theft of the stagecoach. I wonder who the third person is."

George was staring at the ax and the saw which the hijackers had dropped in their haste to get away. "These might be good clues," she remarked. "Fingerprints and that sort of stuff. We'd better not touch them."

"That's right," Nancy agreed.

In a little while the policemen returned, admitting defeat in their pursuit of the hijackers.

Officer Starr smiled. "At least we saved the stolen property," he said, "thanks to you girls."

"Let's right the stagecoach and see what damage has been done to the other side," Nancy suggested.

Five pairs of strong arms soon set the vehicle

back on its wheels. To everyone's delight, practically no damage had been caused.

"This means that the hijackers didn't let it roll off the cliff and land here," said Nancy. "Those men must have brought it down the hillside. If they did," she added, smiling broadly at the two policemen, "the five of us should be able to drag it back up."

The two officers looked at her dubiously but finally consented to try. Bess and George stood on one side of the pole, Nancy on the other. As they grabbed hold, Bess giggled. "This isn't a one-horse shay. It's a three-horse stagecoach!"

Starr and Gavin grinned, then got behind the vehicle and started to shove it. The trip up the slope was an arduous one, but finally the group reached the top. From there out to the main road the task of moving the stagecoach was not difficult.

"I'll be happy to deliver the stagecoach to Mrs. Pauling," Nancy offered.

"All right," said Officer Starr. "Gavin and I will report to headquarters about those hijackers and do more searching for them."

While he radioed to headquarters, Officer Gavin got some heavy rope from his car. The pole of the old stagecoach was firmly tied to the rear bumper of Nancy's convertible.

"If it weren't against the law to ride in a trailer," said Bess, "I'd certainly climb into the old stagecoach."

The three girls finally set off, with Nancy driving very slowly. Motorists along the road stared in amazement and amusement at the sight. Finally Nancy pulled into the Pauling driveway and parked in front of the house.

Mrs. Pauling, who was just coming out of the front door, stared in utter astonishment. Then she cried out, "You found it! Do come inside the house and tell me all about it!"

At that moment George looked at her wrist watch and exclaimed, "Bess, our tennis match is at three o'clock. We'd better dash right off!"

Since it was only twelve thirty, Mrs. Pauling insisted that the girls stay long enough to have lunch. Then she asked whether Nancy would have to go too.

"Not yet," the young sleuth confessed. "As a matter of fact, I'd like to stay and examine the old stagecoach."

"Fine. I'll drive you back to Merriweather later."

While lunch was being prepared, Nancy gave Mrs. Pauling a full report on the recovery of the stagecoach and said she thought they should notify John O'Brien at once. Mrs. Pauling agreed and Nancy put in the call to Bridgeford. The trucker was delighted to learn the good news.

When Nancy returned to the group, Mrs. Pauling said, "The carpenter was here but he left. I'm sure he'll come back if I ask him to." She

phoned Mr. Jennings who promised to return at
two o'clock and carefully take apart the stagecoach piece by piece.

A delicious luncheon of chicken sandwiches,
molded vegetable salad, and tall glasses of lemonade was served in a shaded portion of the patio
garden. As Mrs. Pauling and her guests were eating, the woman asked if the girls were familiar
with the history of stagecoaches. None of them
were.

"It's really very interesting," she said. "The
first stagecoaches used in this country were im-
ported from England, and were called *stage wag-
gons*. But during the War of 1812 the Concord
coach was built in Massachusetts and became very
popular. It was used out West as late as the
1870's."

Bess asked, "Is the stagecoach you bought a
Concord coach?"

"Yes, it is," Mrs. Pauling replied. She chuckled.
"Some record runs were made in those Concord
coaches—twenty miles in forty-five minutes! Con-
sidering the roads in those days, that was marvelous time.

"And speaking of the roads, carriages sank so
deeply in the mud sometimes that the horses
could not pull them out. Getting across creeks,
or bridges that were made of only a few loose
boards, was a real accomplishment."

Bess hunched her shoulders. "I don't think I'd

like to have been on one of those rides," she remarked. "The old stagecoaches must have swayed
around like crazy."

Mrs. Pauling nodded. "Despite that, the stagecoach lines could not carry all the passengers who
wanted to travel. But whenever a railroad came
into a community there were loud complaints
from the stage drivers.

"They were not the only ones who complained,
either. You know the turnpikes and bridges in
those days collected tolls and the owners could see
their profits melting away."

"And I suppose the farmers complained too,"
George spoke up. "Railroads wouldn't buy hay
and grain for their iron horses."

"That's true," Mrs. Pauling agreed. "But as a
matter of fact, the first railroads in this country
used horses. They were the original locomotives
and pulled one or two railway coaches."

By this time Mrs. Pauling and her guests had
finished eating. Bess and George said they really
must leave in order to get back to the lodge in time
to change their clothes and get to the tennis courts.
After thanking their hostess, the girls hurried off.

At two o'clock Mr. Jennings rang the bell and
said he was ready to begin work. The old stagecoach was dragged to a vacant barn at the rear of
the property and the job started.

Mr. Jennings proved to be a talkative individual. "This is one of the best Concord coaches ever

built," he remarked. "See how gracefully the carriage body was slung on these leather straps. They served as springs, you know."

Nancy wished he would hurry taking the stagecoach apart, but he slowly laid out all his tools from a large box and a cloth-wrapped kit which he removed from his car.

"Many laws were passed in connection with the operation of stagecoaches," he went on. "One act of the legislature required lamps to be used on all coaches running at night. Drivers were fined for not doing this. Another regulation was against leaving the horses unfastened while they were hitched to a coach standing still without a driver."

Finally the carpenter settled down to work. First he removed the upholstery from the doors and let Nancy thoroughly examine the padding for any clue which might have been secreted there. She found nothing.

Next he removed the leather backing of the seats, but again the young sleuth had no luck. Then the leather lining of the box under the driver's seat was taken out. There was no clue behind it.

"I guess we'll have to start taking the sections apart," Mr. Jennings said.

Doors came off, the roof was removed, all the seats were taken out, and finally the body was separated from the framework. Wheels and pole were taken off. Still no clue came to light.

"I'm terribly sorry, Miss Drew," Mr. Jennings said. "I know how disappointed you are."

All this time Mrs. Pauling had sat nearby, watching curiously and hopefully. When it became evident that nothing was secreted in the ancient vehicle, Nancy apologized profusely for all the trouble she had caused.

"Please don't worry," Mrs. Pauling said kindly. "I'm only sorry that the little dream which all of us had did not become a reality."

"I admit I'm terribly disappointed," said Nancy. "But I'm not giving up. I've come to this conclusion: We've been investigating the wrong stagecoach. This means I'll have to start all over again and find the right one."

Mrs. Pauling stared at the girl detective. "I certainly admire your perseverance," she said. "But how in the world are you going to find the right stagecoach?"

CHAPTER VII

An Attic Clue

WHEN Nancy returned to her room at the camp, she found Bess and George already in theirs. Quickly stories were exchanged with both sides disappointed in the outcome. Bess and George had lost their tennis match that day.

Nancy smiled. "Too bad. But that will give you all the more time to help me solve my mystery."

"I can see that you already have something in mind," Bess remarked. "Out with it!"

Nancy said she was going to call on Mrs. Strook the following morning. "Now that the mystery has to be tackled from a new angle, I'm hoping she can give me some helpful information."

"Good idea," said George. "Well, let's go and eat. I'm simply starved. That tennis match sure was strenuous."

Directly after dinner a group of young people, including Nancy and her friends, gathered in one corner of the lobby. Conversation was light, as they waited to attend an outdoor movie, to be shown as soon as it was dark.

Nancy was talking with Rick Larrabee when she was rudely interrupted by a woman's voice behind her. "And how did the young sleuth make out today?"

Turning, Nancy looked straight into the eyes of Audrey Monteith. "Oh, very well, thank you," Nancy replied and turned back to talk to Rick.

Audrey, however, was not to be brushed aside easily. "Nancy, don't be so secretive," she scolded. "We'd love to hear about what you've been doing."

Nancy heaved a great sigh, then said as pleasantly as possible, "I really have nothing to tell. I admit I'm trying to solve a mystery, but as yet I haven't done so."

Rick took hold of her arm and led Nancy toward the outdoor movie amphitheater. Taking his cue, the other young people followed close behind and took seats all around Nancy, so that the inquisitive Monteiths could not talk to her.

"You're all dears," Nancy said, chuckling. "Thanks a million."

Early the next morning the young sleuth awakened Bess and George. Nancy said she would like to start off for Mrs. Strook's home before the Monteiths had a chance to follow. Her friends grinned and hurried into their sports clothes. The three girls had breakfast and set off.

They found Mrs. Strook in the front yard, cutting flowers. She greeted her callers with a pleasant good morning, then said, "You must have important news to bring you out so early."

"We plan a full day of sleuthing," Nancy replied, smiling. Then she told Mrs. Strook of her failure regarding the old stagecoach. "I feel sure now that this was not the one your great-uncle owned. What I must do is find the right one."

Mrs. Strook was disappointed, but said she was delighted to know that Nancy would go on with the case. "Have you any idea where to start?" she asked.

"Yes," Nancy answered. "I'd like to know if you have any possessions of Mr. Langstreet—letters, diaries, books, anything to give us a clue."

The elderly woman stood lost in thought for several moments, then said, "I can't think of a single thing that would help, except possibly a diary of my grandfather's. Come into the house and I'll try to find it."

At once the three girls offered to help her search for it. She readily agreed and suggested that Nancy and her friends check the living-room bookcase while she looked in desk drawers. There was silence as the search went on. Ten minutes later all admitted defeat.

"Then my grandfather's old diary must be in the attic," Mrs. Strook concluded. "Let's rest a bit before we go up. In the meantime, I'll show you something I'm rather proud of."

From the desk she pulled out a small book filled with stamps. "Collecting stamps, old and new, from all over the world is a hobby of mine," she said. "A few are rather valuable but they would be more so if they had not been canceled."

The girls looked at page after page, with Mrs. Strook pointing out the fact that *blocks* of uncanceled stamps were the rarest and most expensive of all.

She smiled. "Of course I haven't any of the old ones in blocks or uncanceled."

"Which is your most valuable?" Bess asked.

"This George Washington one of 1847. It's not in very good condition but it's genuine. You know, there are counterfeit stamps on the market."

"How much would a block of four of these genuine George Washingtons be worth if they were uncanceled?" Nancy queried.

"About ten thousand dollars," Mrs. Strook replied.

"Hypers!" George exclaimed.

The elderly woman smiled, closed the book, and put it away. She stood up, saying, "I'm ready to continue our search for the diary now. Suppose you girls follow me upstairs and we'll take a look."

The second floor of the house was as charming

as the first, with its quaint décor and white wood-work. The elderly woman opened a door at the foot of a stairway to the attic and led the way to the very orderly room above.

Trunks and boxes stood in neat rows on one side, while discarded pieces of furniture, includ-ing an old spinning wheel, had been pushed under the eaves along the other three sides. There was no ceiling; just rafters and crossbeams. A few boxes stood on the crossbeams.

Mrs. Strook assigned the girls to various trunks and boxes, while she took others. Bess, who had been given a trunk full of costumes, was intrigued. She wanted to take each one out and hold it up, but knew this would take a lot of time.

Carefully she felt down around the clothing and all over the bottom of the trunk, hoping the old diary might be lying there. But she did not find it. Finally she straightened up and closed the lid of the trunk.

Meanwhile, the other searchers were going through boxes and trunks holding old newspapers, letters, and books. Each was carefully examined, not only for the diary, but for some advertisement, a letter slipped between the pages, or a marked passage in some volume that would give a hint about Great-uncle Abner Langstreet's intentions. Nothing was found.

Finally Mrs. Strook suggested a rest period and sat down on an old-fashioned chair. Bess offered to go downstairs and bring up glasses of water for Mrs. Strook and the others. She could see that the woman was becoming very weary and suggested that she lie down on an antique sofa.

"All right," she said. "But you strong young people go on with the search. I've forgotten what is in those boxes up on the crossbeams."

After Bess had brought the water and the searchers had drained their glasses, the girls began work again. Each took one of the boxes on the crossbeams and started to pull it toward her. Nancy's was very heavy and difficult to move. She stood on tiptoe and tugged at it. Little by little the box inched along toward the edge.

Suddenly, as she gave it an extra tug, the box turned upside down and fell directly on her head! Stunned, she let go of it and slumped to the floor.

"Oh, Nancy!" Bess cried out fearfully. She dashed to her friend's side.

George, too, was there in a jiffy. Mrs. Strook had arisen from the sofa and hurried forward. "Oh dear! Oh dear!" she wailed. "I hope it's nothing serious!"

"I'm sure it's not," George tried to reassure the elderly woman, who had become ghostly pale.

Nancy was murmuring. She opened her eyes and reached one hand to the top of her head. Already a bump was starting to form.

"That was a nasty crack you got," said George. "I'll go down and get some ice to put on it." She hurried down the stairs to the kitchen and returned in less than a minute with ice cubes wrapped in a towel.

By this time Nancy was seated on the sofa, and declared that she would be all right in a few moments. She was relieved, however, to have the ice pack to reduce the swelling on her head. But soon her good humor returned and she remarked facetiously:

"I'll have to change my hair-do for a couple of days to hide this bump!"

The others laughed and Mrs. Strook in particular felt relieved to know that Nancy was all right. Nevertheless, she shook her head, saying, "It's wonderful the way you young people can make such quick comebacks."

The contents of the box Nancy had pulled down were strewn on the floor. Suddenly Mrs. Strook saw her grandfather's diary. Picking it up, she began thumbing through the old book.

"Here are some items that may help you," she said excitedly. "It tells about my grandfather's endeavor to trace his brother-in-law. He contacted every stagecoach line in the country and he had also written to every driver of a private stagecoach whose name he could learn. But no one could tell him anything about Great-uncle Abner's stagecoach."

Mrs. Strook continued to read to herself from the diary. The girls did not interrupt. In a few moments she said, "Here's another item. My grandfather also contacted all the old inns and taverns located along the stagecoach routes. Abner Langstreet never registered at any of them."

"Well, that eliminates the idea that Mr. Langstreet sold the stagecoach out West," George remarked. "It looks as if he must have hidden it somewhere around here."

"Yes, it does," Mrs. Strook agreed. She sighed. "But maybe by this time the coach has rotted away and we'll never find it."

Nancy, determined not to lose hope, said, "It's my hunch that if Mr. Abner Langstreet loved his stagecoach as much as I've been led to believe, he would do everything he could to preserve it. I'm sure that it's hidden away safely somewhere. He intended to tell in the letter he wrote to your grandmother, Mrs. Strook, where he had put it, but I believe he died without having a chance to do so."

Mrs. Strook smiled fondly at Nancy. "You're such a wonderful girl," she said.

"If you're right, Nancy," said Bess, "where do we go from here?"

Nancy had a quick answer. "To the place where Mr. Abner Langstreet spent his last days."

CHAPTER VIII

A Whistler's Confession

"PERHAPS you'll go with us, Mrs. Strook," Nancy invited. But the elderly woman said she did not feel physically able to make the trip to her great-uncle's last home.

"Can you show me on a map exactly where it is?" the young sleuth went on.

When Mrs. Strook nodded, Nancy offered to bring a road map from her car. The whole group returned to the living room. As Nancy hurried outdoors, she noticed a truck parked just back of her automobile. Drawing closer, she recognized the driver as Judd Hillary!

As soon as he saw Nancy, the unpleasant man alighted. Facing her, he said angrily, "I've been waitin' for you."

"Yes?" Nancy asked in surprise.

"I gave you a warnin', young lady, but you're not payin' any attention to it," Judd Hillary said harshly. "Can't you keep that nose o' yours out o' other people's business? You don't live around here. You don't pay taxes. You just come up here to have a good time. Well, why don't you stick to that? You don't have to go runnin' around messin' in the affairs o' our place!"

"I wasn't aware that I was doing such a thing," said Nancy coolly.

She planned to ignore the man, but he followed her to the convertible. It suddenly occurred to Nancy that he probably had posted himself there to see what she was doing and where she was going. It might be best not to pull out the map at this time.

Suddenly Judd Hillary burst out, "What did you do with the old stagecoach?"

Nancy was so amazed at the question that she stared dumfounded. But she was instantly on her guard. In reply she said, "Mr. Hillary, why are you so interested in the old stagecoach?"

The man had a ready answer. "Because you are," he said. "You can't hide anything from me. You're workin' for the opposition. They're an underhanded bunch. They got somethin' up their sleeves. If they set you onto examinin' the old stagecoach, it means somethin'. I want to know what it is!"

Nancy wondered how she was going to get rid of the man. She was a bit puzzled by his attitude. On the one hand he seemed genuinely interested in keeping the local taxes and those of surrounding communities from being raised. On the other hand, the very fact that he had learned she was interested in examining the old stagecoach could even mean he knew the hijackers!

"I wonder how I can find out," she asked herself. Then an idea came to her and she decided on a bold move. Looking directly at him, she said, "Mr. Hillary, you whistle very well."

The tall, muscular man fell back. "How do you know that I can—?" Then he interrupted himself abruptly and the momentary look of fright which had come over his face vanished. Setting his jaw, he said, "You never heard me whistle, so what are you talking about?"

Nancy did not answer. She felt positive that Judd Hillary had given himself away: He had some connection with the hijackers!

Having proved that fact to herself, she decided on a new tack to disarm him. "Yes, I felt that there was something very valuable hidden in that old stagecoach. But I was wrong. It has all been taken apart and thoroughly searched. Not a thing was found." She smiled at Judd Hillary. "So you won't have to worry about it any longer."

The man gave Nancy a searching look as if he could not make up his mind whether or not to believe her. Finally he mumbled something to himself she could not hear.

In a louder voice he said, "I'm warnin' you

again. Don't be pokin' into the business o' other people!"

He got into his truck, started the motor, and jerkily drove up the street.

Nancy gazed after him wonderingly. "So he was the whistler!" she told herself. "That is a clue I'm certainly going to pursue."

Nancy opened the car door and found the road map. Returning to the house, she spread it out on Mrs. Strook's dining-room table. She pointed to Francisville and then asked the elderly woman if she could locate the spot where Abner Langstreet had spent his last days.

It took Mrs. Strook some time to figure this out. At last she put her finger on an area about half a mile in from a side road marked 123A. "I think this is the place."

"There's a private road leading to the farm?" George asked.

"I believe so," Mrs. Strook said. "I have never been on it myself, but I'm told it's only a dirt road."

She warned the girls that this was a desolate area.

"Does anyone live on the farm now?" Nancy asked.

"Oh, yes. In fact, people have lived on the place ever since Great-uncle Abner passed away. But no one has improved the farm much. I understand that right now a young couple are living on it. They're having a struggle financially."

"That's a shame," said Bess sympathetically.

Mrs. Strook nodded. "Their name is Zucker. I believe the husband was advised by a doctor to live on a farm for health reasons. Mr. Zucker is feeling better but knows little about farming, so it's difficult to make ends meet."

The elderly woman wished the girls luck as Nancy folded up the map and said they must go. At that moment all of them heard thunder. Flashes of lightning streaked across the sky.

"Oh, you must stay until the storm is over," Mrs. Strook insisted.

"I guess we'd better," said Nancy. "I'll run out and put up the top of my car."

Rain came down in torrents for about twenty minutes, then slackened off slightly. The thunder and lightning ceased, but the rain continued.

"I'm afraid," said Mrs. Strook, "that it will rain all the rest of the day. I'd advise you girls not to try going out to the Zucker place. You'd certainly get stuck on those bad roads."

Nancy realized the wisdom of this. "I'll take your advice, Mrs. Strook," she said, "and make the trip tomorrow."

The girls said good-by and dashed through the rain to the convertible. As Nancy turned it left upon reaching Main Street, and Bess realized that they were headed for the business section of Francisville rather than Camp Merriweather, she inquired the reason. Nancy told of her recent clash with Judd Hillary outside Mrs. Strook's house.

"Oh, how dreadful!" Bess exclaimed. "You really think Judd Hillary is mixed up with those hijackers?"

As Nancy nodded, George remarked, "Since Judd Hillary knows you're an amateur detective, he has no doubt told that to those crooks."

Bess agreed, and added worriedly, "We've never even heard their names. When you know who your enemies are it's bad enough, but when you don't—well, it gives me the shivers to think about it."

Nancy remarked, "Since I told Judd Hillary no clue had been found in the old stagecoach, I believe they'll leave me alone."

"I certainly hope so," said Bess. "And what are we going to do in Francisville?"

"First, quiz the druggist, Mr. Benfield, then other shopkeepers to learn if any of them ever saw Judd Hillary with two tall men, one a blond and the other dark with a scar across his left wrist."

Bess and George offered to help. By the time they were ready to start their inquiry, the rain had let up enough for them to dodge from place to place without getting too wet. They agreed to meet at the Willow Tearoom for a late lunch.

When the three girls gathered together again,

each reported failure. "I suppose that proves," said George, "that Judd Hillary meets these friends of his out in the country where nobody will see them." Nancy nodded.

After the girls had eaten, they found that the rain was still coming down fitfully so Nancy, Bess, and George decided to return to the lodge. Here they found that the management had arranged an eight-o'clock dinner dance. Tables had been taken from the center of the dining-room floor and only a ring of them left around the edges.

Nancy, Bess, and George also learned that the special group whom they dated, Rick, Jack Smith, and Hobe White, had engaged a long table with places for the three girls. Dressed in pretty frocks, Nancy in blue, George in deep yellow, and Bess in pale green, the girls arrived in the lobby just before eight.

Rick and the other two boys immediately came up to them and together they walked into the dining room. The rest of their group was already there. They also found Ross and Audrey Monteith dragging chairs from another table with the thought of joining them.

Rick scowled. Going up to the couple, he told them that there were no places left at the table. "Oh, two more won't hurt," Audrey argued, trying to smile bewitchingly but failing completely.

"It is already crowded," said Rick, his eyes flashing.

"Now you know," Ross spoke up, "that there's always room for two more."

"In this case there's not," Rick said with such finality that the Monteiths pulled their chairs back to the other table.

"Good for you," Nancy whispered to her partner. Soon the first course was served and the music started. She forgot all about the unpleasant couple.

The rain had stopped several hours before and about ten o'clock the moon came up. Nancy and Rick, after a dance, strolled outside into the lovely garden. Deep in conversation, they walked to the very end of it.

"One more year of college, then I'll be a full-fledged engineer," Rick remarked. "I can hardly wait to get out and start work."

Before Nancy had a chance to comment, she and Rick became aware of someone walking in the woods beyond the end of the garden. They stopped to listen. The other person had paused also, but now they could hear a faint clicking noise.

"What is that?" Nancy whispered.

Rick listened a few seconds, then he said in surprise, "It sounds like a Geiger counter. But who in the world would be hunting uranium ore or other metals around here?"

CHAPTER IX

Trouble on the Road

NANCY started toward the woods to investigate the strange clicking sound.

Rick followed. "You'd better stay here," he cautioned her. "I'll go."

Just then the clicking ceased and Ross Monteith emerged from among the trees! He was carrying a cane!

"Oh!" Ross cried out as he almost ran into the couple. "I didn't see you!"

"Have you taken to walking alone in the woods after dark?" Rick asked him.

Ross Monteith laughed lightly. "I had a good old flashlight to help me." He tapped his jacket pocket. "Audrey thought she'd lost one of her favorite earrings in the woods this morning and I offered to try to find it for her. No luck, though."

As Ross started to move off, Nancy asked him,

"Did you hear a peculiar clicking noise while you were in the woods?"

"Clicking noise?" he repeated. "No, I didn't. Why?"

"Oh, we thought we did and wondered what it was."

"Sorry I can't help you," Ross said, and hurried off.

Nancy and Rick discussed the whole episode. It was evident from their frowns that neither of them quite believed what Monteith had said. Why had he been in the woods? And was he telling the truth about not hearing the clicking noise?

Rick suddenly chuckled. "Nancy," he said, "how about this deduction from a novice at sleuthing? I think Ross Monteith's cane contains a Geiger counter. After dark he goes around prospecting for valuable minerals."

Nancy laughed. "Well," she said, "your theory is more comforting than having the cane turn out to be a deadly weapon!"

Long after Nancy had gone to bed that evening, she continued to think about the various angles of the mystery which she was trying to solve. Two questions concerning the Monteiths kept recurring to her mind. Were the couple just being nuisances? Or was there more to their always trying to be wherever Nancy was?

As the young sleuth was finally falling asleep, she decided to stay out of the couple's way as much as possible. "And I'll warn Bess and George not to say anything in front of them which would give away any of our plans."

Nancy awoke early the next day and decided at once on one way to start her campaign of secrecy. She would move her car from the parking lot to a little-used side road a short distance from the lodge. "Then Ross and Audrey can't spy on me so easily."

She dressed quickly and went outside. No one was around. Nancy drove off, but was back at the lodge on foot within fifteen minutes.

Bess and George were just waking up. Nancy told them what she had done, and also her suspicions about the Monteiths.

"They haven't really done anything," she said, "but I think it would be just as well to throw them off our trail if possible."

"It sure would," said George. "The thing for us to do is get out of this hotel without their seeing us. What say we dress for tennis after breakfast and head for the courts, but carry skirts and purses in our beach bags?"

"Good idea," Nancy agreed.

When the girls reached the tennis courts, only the boy who put up nets was there. He was so busy with his chore that he did not even notice Nancy and her friends, who avoided the courts, went through a trail that led out to the main road, and on down to Nancy's car. Here they put on their skirts, then set off in the open car. Bess suddenly giggled. "This is like playing hare and hounds in reverse. Usually we're the hounds. This time we're the hares."

Nancy asked George to get the map out of the instrument-panel compartment. "Tell me when I'm nearing that road which Mrs. Strook penciled in," she requested.

Nancy drove for several miles, turning from one road to another, trying to get to the exact spot. It was very confusing but at last George cried out:

"Here's a road—that is, if you can call it a road. I'm sure this is the right one."

The one-car lane was rutty, bumpy, and full of stones. As rocks banged against the under part of the chassis, Nancy slowed to a crawl. In many places the grass in the road was so tall that George declared it was like driving through a wheat field. The girls were joggled from side to side.

Finally Bess said she thought it was foolhardy to go on. "Nancy, we'll break a spring on the car or do some other damage," she declared.

"I agree with you," Nancy replied. "But I can't turn around here. I'll have to go on until I come to a wider spot. You notice it's kind of mucky along the edges here—I guess from that rain yesterday. I'm afraid we'd get stuck."

There was a sharp turn a short distance farther on and just beyond it the girls found themselves confronted by a chain across the road. From it hung a sign, on which was printed in large letters:

UNITED STATES
GOVERNMENT PROPERTY
KEEP OUT!

"They certainly don't want any visitors here," Bess remarked. "This must be an experimental station of some kind."

Nancy had a hard time getting her convertible turned around. She had to do it inches at a time. But finally she was headed in the opposite direction and started the jolting ride back to the main road.

"Since this wasn't the right road," said Bess, "I wonder where the one to the Zucker farm is. We might be miles from it."

Nancy disagreed. "Mrs. Strook seemed so sure of the spot, I believe we'll find the road not far from here."

"I hope it isn't as bad as this one," Bess worried, as she suddenly flew off the seat. "I'd better stop talking or I'll bite my tongue!" she added with a giggle as she landed.

Bess had no sooner said this when the car stopped abruptly. The engine had died.

"Goodness, what's the matter?" Bess asked.

Nancy's eyes had darted to the fuel tank. "It's empty—completely empty!"

"But you just had the tank filled while we were in Francisville," George told her.

Bess gave an earsplitting scream

"I know," Nancy replied. "It's my guess that one of the rocks we went over punctured a hole in the tank."

"And all our gas is gone?" Bess exclaimed in dismay.

"I'm afraid so," Nancy told her.

The girls got out of the car and looked back of them. There was a long trail of gasoline on the grass-covered road.

"This is a fine predicament!" said Bess. "Here we are in the middle of nowhere. What are we going to do?" Just then she glanced up and gave an earsplitting scream. *"Look!"*

Nancy and George glanced up just in time to see a large black bear, its teeth bared, loping toward them. He was not more than fifty feet away!

CHAPTER X

Secret Notes

IN A flash the three girls jumped inside the car and Nancy pushed the buttons for the mechanisms to raise the top and the windows. The job was finished just as the shaggy black bear reached them.

"Oh, I hope he won't get nasty and break the windows," Bess said, fright in her voice.

The bruin stood up on its hind legs and sniffed the car. Then he got down and walked round and round it, grunting.

"We're virtually prisoners," said George. "We might be here for days!"

Nancy chuckled. "The bear is bound to get hungry at some time and go off looking for food."

"He might decide not to," said Bess. "He'd probably find us a good meal."

"Don't be silly," George chided her cousin. "Bears like honey and green things—"

Bess was unconvinced. "Well, even if he didn't eat us, he could maul us to death."

Each time the bear had stood on its hind legs to peer inside the car, Nancy had looked intently at the fur around his neck. Finally she detected what she was looking for—a collar.

"I believe this fellow is tame and has escaped from some place," she said.

George grinned. "You mean he's lonesome and wants to crawl in here with us?" She pretended to open the door, whereupon Bess gave one of her loudest screams.

"His master's probably looking for him," said Nancy. "I'll sound the horn to attract his attention."

She began a series of staccato blasts and in about ten minutes the girls saw a man coming down the road. He was wearing a white shirt, riding breeches, and puttees. As he drew nearer, the bear loped up to him. He patted the animal, took a stout chain from his pocket, and slipped it into a ring on the bear's collar. Then the two of them walked over to the car. By this time Nancy had lowered the windows.

"I'm sorry Sally frightened you," the man said. "She got away while I was dozing after lunch."

He introduced himself as Harold Henderson and said he was transporting Sally from one county fair to another. "Thanks for sounding the horn," he said, smiling.

Nancy grinned back. "I'm afraid we had a double reason for doing so. We need a little help ourselves." She explained about the hole in the gas tank.

"Well, one good turn deserves another," Harold Henderson said. "I'll take Sally back to the truck, lock her up so she can't get out again, and then come back here with putty. It'll fix up that hole temporarily. I'll bring some gas too."

He started off.

"We're just plain lucky," Bess remarked, as the girls sat and waited. "I hope that we'll be as lucky finding the Zucker farm."

Harold Henderson returned in a little while, puttied the hole, then covered it with tire tape.

"I'm sure that'll hold till you get to a service station," he said, and poured half a gallon of gasoline from a can into the tank.

He refused to take any money from Nancy. "My help," he said, "is a small return for your aid in recovering my bear. The loss of her would have meant many dollars out of my pocket tonight."

He hopped aboard the convertible and it started up the road. Nancy went very carefully, and when she reached the main road, turned right at Mr. Henderson's direction. Soon they came to his truck where Sally sat on her haunches, looking around. She seemed very content.

"You'll find a service station about half a mile

down this road," Henderson said. "It's at the junction of one of the main highways."

When Nancy reached the service station, the temporary work was replaced with a permanent repair job. Then the tank was filled.

While the mechanic worked on the car, Nancy asked him if he knew anyone in the neighborhood named Zucker. "A young couple with a baby?" he queried.

"They live on an isolated farm."

"They're the ones all right," the garageman replied. "I don't know why they want to live back there. Ground's full of rocks. Not many fields on it to farm. Zucker can't make money that way."

Nancy asked for specific directions and was told to continue straight ahead for another half mile. "Then, if you look sharp, you will see a lane. It's just about the width of a car. The Zuckers get in and out all right, so I guess you can. But it's rough going. The house is about half a mile in."

The girls started off again and presently found the trail. Nancy turned in and drove slowly, mostly through woods, until she came to the Zucker property. It was evident that the original house had been a one-room structure to which an addition had been built fairly recently.

The callers noticed a baby's net-covered play pen in the dooryard. In it was an infant asleep.

A young couple came from the house and

smiled at the girls, who stepped out of the car. "Are you looking for us—the Zuckers?" the man asked.

Nancy revealed why they had come and asked if he could give her any information about the old stagecoach which Abner Langstreet had driven.

"I'm afraid not," the young man replied, introducing himself as Morton and his wife as Marjory. Nancy introduced herself and the other two girls.

Marjory spoke up, "When we moved here, this place had been thoroughly cleaned out. Oh, there was plenty of dirt, but not even a bottle or a piece of firewood or anything."

"And former owners never mentioned anything about Abner Langstreet living here or owning a stagecoach?" Nancy asked.

The Zuckers shook their heads, then Morton said, "But if you think you can find anything, you're more than welcome to look around."

"Thank you," said Nancy. "Actually, I was hoping there might be a bill of sale of the old stagecoach hidden away, perhaps behind some secret panel."

Intrigued, the Zuckers said they would like to join in a search. First an ancient barn was thoroughly searched. Nothing came to light.

"What was that old shed used for?" Nancy asked.

"I believe it was the blacksmith shop," Morton answered. "A hundred years ago life on a farm was very different from today. A man was his own blacksmith and builder as well as farmer. Besides growing all his own grain, fruits, and vegetables, and raising chickens, colts, calves, and pigs, he built houses and barns, with some help from his neighbors."

"Amazing," Bess murmured.

"The farmer also forged and hammered his own iron hardware for nails, latches, andirons, and lamp bases," Morton went on. "He often made wrought-iron boxes and tools," the young man ended, as they entered the shed.

Marjory smiled. "I guess that's how the saying started, 'A man works from sun to sun.'"

No clues were found in the shed, so Morton said, "Let's try the house."

On the way there, Morton added suddenly, "I just thought of something. When I bought this farm I had the title thoroughly searched. Abner Langstreet was never an owner, so if he lived here he must have rented the place."

"I'm sure that's true," said Nancy. "If the property were registered at the courthouse, Abner Langstreet could have been found."

"Maybe this isn't the right place," said Bess.

Nancy reminded her that Mrs. Strook had given the directions, and if the Zuckers were willing, she thought they should go on with the search. Morton insisted that they do so.

"I'm highly interested in this thing myself

now," he said. "A missing stagecoach!" He looked quizzically at Nancy. "You didn't say so, but I figure there must be something valuable hidden inside it."

"We suspect there may be," Nancy confessed, but did not explain further.

Work began in the four-room farmhouse. It was decided to confine the search to the original building. Walls were carefully tapped, and the stones of the fireplace inspected for any which might pull out. The hunt proved futile.

"Do you mind if I peek under your rugs, Marjory?" Nancy asked, "to see if there might be an old trap door or loose board?"

"Go ahead," the farmer's wife said. "And I wish you luck!"

Nancy looked under each of the small hooked rugs which lay on the wide-board floor. She was about to give up and admit defeat, when one of the boards seemed unsteady as she trod back and forth on it. "There may be something under here!" she called out excitedly.

Morton brought a small wedge from a tool chest in the kitchen and pried up one end of the board.

"Why, there are lots of notes underneath!" Bess exclaimed.

The notes, in an old-fashioned handwriting, had been placed in rows on top of a board lying on the ground. They were musty but legible. Without disturbing them, Nancy began to read the words.

The first one in the upper left-hand corner read, "First burial today." The one directly below it said, "Second burial today." To the onlookers' amazement the same phrase with succeeding numerals appeared on each of the notes, which numbered thirty.

"Ugh!" Bess cried out. "This is gruesome!"

Marjory Zucker was greatly disturbed. Turning to her husband, she said, "Morton, there may be a graveyard on our property!"

By this time Nancy had picked up the first note and turned it over. On the back was written Abner Langstreet, October 1, 1853.

"This *was* Great-uncle Abner's hide-out!" the young sleuth cried out excitedly.

Each note was turned over. All were signed with the same signature, and each was dated one day later than the note before it. On a few of them were short lines and here and there a circle.

Morton Zucker had put an arm around his wife. "I am sure if there is a burial ground on this property, it was not for human beings. Probably Mr. Langstreet had to shoot various wild animals for self-protection and buried them one by one."

"Possibly," Nancy agreed. "But there may be some other explanation. One thing I do know. If these notes were really written by Abner Langstreet, they were done only one month after he disappeared from Francisville."

She went on to say that she thought the handwriting should be compared with something which Abner Langstreet had written. "May I borrow these notes?" she asked Morton. "I'd like to take them to Mrs. Strook. She may have a sample of her great-uncle's handwriting, and we can compare it with these notes."

"Take them along," the young man said. He smiled. "They're certainly no good to me."

Before the girls left, the Zuckers invited them to come back at any time and make a further search. Morton grinned. "Maybe I won't even wait for you," he said. "I may do some searching and find the old stagecoach."

"Please do," Nancy answered. "And if you locate anything, call me at Camp Merriweather."

"I sure will."

On the way to Mrs. Strook's home, the three girls discussed the mystery from this new angle.

"Do you think the notes are authentic?" Bess asked Nancy.

"Yes, I do. And I believe they prove without a doubt that Mr. Langstreet never went out West to sell his stagecoach. He wouldn't have had time to get there and back before October 1, 1853. The coach must be hidden in this very area!"

"Maybe," Bess said. "But the vehicle was so large, how could he have hidden it without someone having found it during the past hundred years?"

"I have a theory," Nancy replied. "I think from what the notes say that Great-uncle Abner took his stagecoach apart piece by piece and lovingly buried them somewhere day after day."

"But wouldn't they have rotted away by this time?" George argued.

"They might have," said Nancy, "but I have a feeling Mr. Langstreet would somehow have protected the stagecoach, particularly if it contained something valuable."

Bess asked if Nancy was going to dig up the Zucker farm to try finding it.

"I may," the young sleuth replied. "But even if we find the coach, the clue in it may not be of any value to the town of Francisville."

"Why not?" Bess asked.

Nancy said that anything located on the Zucker property would belong to them as owners.

Bess and George groaned. "Why, Mrs. Strook would be heartbroken!"

"Yes, I'm afraid she would," Nancy replied. "But we'll have to— Oh!" she cried out.

The car wheel had been almost wrenched from her hand by a sudden violent tremor of the ground. This was accompanied by an explosion not far away!

CHAPTER XI

The Cave-in

"IT's an earthquake!" Bess cried out, as Nancy swerved her car to keep it from going into a ditch. "Please let's stop and get out!"

Nancy turned off the engine and the three girls hopped to the road. There was no further tremor of the earth.

"There must have been blasting some place near here," George remarked.

The girls climbed into the convertible again and Nancy drove on. About half a mile farther along they found a crowd of people gathering. The center of the explosion seemed to have been at this point and everyone was trying to find out the cause.

"Folks have no business using dynamite or bombs without permission," said an irate man, "and I happen to know that not a soul applied for a license to do this."

Nancy and her friends joined the search in a long field for the person or persons responsible. As they hurried along Bess asked if Nancy had any theory regarding the explosion.

"We're not far from the end of one of those housing developments," the young sleuth whispered. "This might have been a bomb scare to get people to move out."

"You mean," said George in a low voice, "that somebody like Judd Hillary or one of his backers might have done it?"

"I'm not making any accusations," Nancy replied. "But I think it would be a good idea if we keep our eyes open for suspicious-looking persons."

The three girls did not notice any such person at first, but just as the group reached a tremendous cave-in of earth caused by the recent explosion, they saw Judd Hillary. Nancy and her chums edged near him. He was talking to a group and wore a self-satisfied smirk.

"Now maybe this'll drive some o' those newcomers away," he was saying.

Bess winked at Nancy, who walked up to the man. "Mr. Hillary, just why are you against progress in this community?" she asked.

The man became livid with rage. "You already know the answer and besides you don't belong around here. Why don't you get out and stop snoopin'!"

This crude remark angered Nancy. "No, I don't live here," she said. "But I do have a lot of sympathy for people who are in danger."

"Yes," George broke in, "instead of feeling relieved that no one was hurt by the explosion, you seem delighted that it happened. You say you don't want newcomers here because of higher taxes, but there are some people who think you have other reasons for keeping them out which you're not telling!"

Judd Hillary fell back as if he had been stunned. He seemed at a loss for an answer and a frightened look had come over his face. But he recovered quickly. Throwing back his head, he said disdainfully:

"You got no business talkin' like that. I don't have to say any more. Your friend here has had a couple of warnings. Now I'll give you one: *Leave this place before you get hurt!*"

At that moment two men stepped forward and took hold of Judd Hillary's arms. As they began telling him that this was no way to talk to young ladies who were spending a vacation in the neighborhood, Nancy whispered to her friends to follow her. She threaded her way through the crowd, saying, "Maybe those two hijackers are in this with Hillary! Let's look for them!"

The girls circled the crowd from the rear but did not find the two suspects. Nancy was about to give up when George spotted two men she thought might be the hijackers running toward the road. The girls darted after them. But before they could get close enough to identify the two or read the license plate of a car into which they jumped, the men drove off at top speed.

"Here come the police," Bess spoke up.

Four officers alighted from a squad car and hurried toward the crowd that had gathered at the site of the explosion. Nancy and her friends followed the policemen. But the officers announced that everyone who could not give them any clue as to who had caused the explosion was to leave.

"I guess that includes us," said George.

"Maybe not," said Nancy. "Our clue about Hillary and the hijackers is a pretty slim one, but I think we should tell the police my suspicions."

She waited until everyone else had gone, then told the officers who she was and what was in her mind.

"Thank you, Miss Drew," one of them said. "I'll report this to the chief. I heard about the stagecoach hijacking. You may have a good clue this time too."

Nancy nodded and the three girls left. Once more they climbed into Nancy's convertible and headed for Mrs. Strook's home. They found the elderly woman in a highly nervous state over the explosion. Nancy tried to reassure her, saying everything was all right now.

"But it was most frightening," said Mrs. Strook.

"And come, I want to show you what happened."

She led them into her dining room where there were several triangular shelves in a corner. On some stood prized pieces of antique glass and porcelain. But many others had crashed to the floor and broken into hundreds of pieces.

"Some of these were priceless," said Mrs. Strook. "They have been in my family for several generations."

The girls expressed their sympathy and George added practically, "I'm glad it wasn't you, Mrs. Strook, who fell and was injured."

Nancy smiled and said, "I have a nice surprise to tell you about. Suppose I make some hot tea and we'll sit down and talk things over." While Nancy fixed the tea, the other girls swept up the broken pieces of porcelain.

After the elderly woman had had a cup of tea and some homemade cookies, she declared she felt calmer and wanted to know what Nancy had to tell her.

"I hope it's a clue to my great-uncle's stagecoach," she said wistfully.

"Yes, it is," Nancy replied. From her purse she took out one of the strange notes found under the floor at the Zucker farm and handed it to Mrs. Strook. "Is that Mr. Langstreet's handwriting?" she asked.

"Why, I believe it is," the woman answered. "I can easily prove it. I have been doing some searching here and came across a letter which Great-uncle Abner wrote to my grandmother not long before he disappeared. I'll get it."

Nancy had not shown Mrs. Strook the reverse side of the note with its morbid words. The young sleuth decided to wait until later before discussing this.

When Mrs. Strook returned from the second floor, she was holding a small letter written in a cramped hand and now very faded. Quickly the two signatures were compared.

"There's no question the same person made both of these," Nancy cried excitedly. She noted, however, that the one she had brought was very shaky compared to the other. When writing the "burial" notes Mr. Langstreet had no doubt been under a great emotional strain.

"Nancy," said Mrs. Strook, "tell me again where you found the notes."

The young detective brought out all thirty notes and turned over several of them. When the elderly woman read the messages, she gave an involuntary shudder.

"What do you think they mean?" she asked.

Nancy explained her theory about the old stage-coach being lovingly taken apart, the sections put into containers to preserve them, and with great ceremony buried box by box.

"I think it may have been right on the farm where he was living," Nancy explained. "But if so, there's one angle to it which worries me. The Zuckers can claim the coach and also anything valuable found with it."

Mrs. Strook was silent a few moments, then she said bravely, "We'll have to take that chance, Nancy. Perhaps it's just intuition, but I have a strong feeling that the clue my great-uncle mentioned has no connection with the Zucker property."

"But suppose the stagecoach is on somebody else's property?" George remarked. "Then the person who owns that place can claim it, can't he?"

"I suppose so," said Mrs. Strook. "Oh dear, what do you think we'd better do?"

"I have another idea," said Nancy. "Where else did any member of your family own property in this area? The old stagecoach may be there."

Mrs. Strook went to a desk and brought out a large old-fashioned map. It revealed that Abner Langstreet's father had owned a tremendous amount of land in the vicinity of Francisville. He had divided it into parcels, giving one to each of his sons and daughters.

"And he had eleven children!" said Mrs. Strook.

She went on to explain that three of the sections were still owned by members of the family, but the other eight had been sold.

Nancy, seeing that Mrs. Strook was becoming downhearted, said with a smile, "Let's not worry about that just now. I believe we should keep on trying to solve the mystery. Don't you agree, Mrs. Strook?"

"Indeed I do!" the woman said with spirit. "And I do hope it will be soon. I can hardly sleep nights thinking about it."

On the way back to Camp Merriweather, Nancy was unusually silent and serious. Bess and George chatted but Nancy did not offer a word of conversation. She was mentally pursuing several new ideas, but always coming to a dead end.

When the three girls reached their rooms, Bess closed the door between them. Nancy was so intent with her thoughts that she did not notice.

"George," Bess said in a low voice, "Nancy's in the doldrums. We must get her out of them."

"I agree, but how?"

"Listen," said Bess, and with a giggle whispered something into George's ear.

Her cousin's face broke into a broad grin. "Swell!" she said. "We'll do it!"

CHAPTER XII

Shadowing

IN HER own room, Nancy almost automatically took a shower and dressed for dinner. There was to be dancing that evening in the garden on a platform built at one side. She decided to wear a summer cotton of yellow and white and rather tailored in design. She put on white slippers with medium-height heels.

When she was ready, the young detective lay down on the bed while waiting for Bess and George to open the door between their rooms. Nancy mulled over the mystery from every angle.

"I hate to admit it, but it has me stymied at the moment," she told herself.

Just then someone knocked on her door. Raising herself up and swinging her feet to the floor, Nancy called out, "Come in!"

The hall door swung wide. Nancy's eyes popped in surprise, then she burst into laughter.

In walked Bess and George, rigged out to look like Audrey and Ross Monteith. Bess as Audrey had her hair pulled high and tight on top of her head with a mop of curls at the crown. She wore an extremely tight-fitting sports dress of George's. Her cheeks and lips were very artificially red and her fingernails looked as if they had been dipped in garnet paint. She swaggered in on her extremely high-heeled shoes.

George's outfit was even funnier. She wore baggy slacks, which belonged to Bess, a white shirt, and a very loud sports jacket borrowed from Jack Smith. She swung a cane and kept blinking her eyes at nothing, exactly the way Ross Monteith did when he was assuming an affected pose.

"Beg pawdon, Nancy," said "Mr. Monteith," "but I'd be jolly pleased if you would tell me your plans for the evening."

"Oh, yes," added "Mrs. Monteith," "Rossy and I don't like secrets. We'd prefer being with you wherever you go."

Nancy was giggling merrily. She got up from the bed and gave the door a slight push to close it. Then she sat down again.

"Oh, Audrey," said "Ross," opening a little box in which Nancy kept her costume jewelry, "heah are some perfectly stunning earrings. I'm sure Nancy would be glad to lend them to you in place of the ones you lost in the woods." George spun the cane in a circle.

"Audrey" gave a sinister chuckle. "And maybe —just maybe—I shan't return them," Bess said. She took the earrings out of the box.

At that very moment Nancy's eyes traveled toward the door to the hall. She thought she had heard a sound outside. Eavesdroppers?

Nancy tiptoed across the room and yanked the door open. Ross and Audrey Monteith stood there! Nancy was not sure whether their look of surprise had been caused by her opening the door so suddenly or because they had been caught eavesdropping. Their look of amazement lasted only a couple of seconds, however.

Then Audrey bubbled, "We came to ask—" Suddenly she looked at Bess and George. "For Pete's sake, what—"

None of the three girls explained the little skit. If the Monteiths had heard themselves being ridiculed, Nancy and her friends hoped it would be a good lesson to them. If they had not, then there was no point in telling them.

When the callers realized they were not to be told what was going on, Ross Monteith changed the subject. "We came to ask you to help us get up a hayride. I think it would be a lot of fun, don't you? Audrey and I thought the five of us might take tomorrow off and drive around the countryside looking for a farmer who has horses and an old-fashioned hayrack."

"It sounds like a lot of fun," Nancy remarked.

"But I couldn't possibly help you make any arrangements."

"You have a previous engagement?" Ross asked quickly.

The young sleuth was sure that the man was angling for information about her plans. She decided to give him none, and hoped that neither Bess nor George would speak up.

"I have so many things to do," Nancy said, "I don't know which ones to do first. With tennis and swimming and horseback riding here—" She did not finish the sentence and for a few seconds there was silence in the room.

George decided this was an opportune time to get rid of the visitors. She looked at her wrist watch. "My goodness, Bess, we'd better jump out of this gear in a hurry and get ready for dinner or we'll be late."

"Yes," Bess agreed. She giggled. "That wouldn't do at all because I'm starved."

As George opened the door between the two rooms, Audrey and Ross Monteith started to sit down. This was not to Nancy's liking!

Quickly she said, "Sorry I can't talk to you any longer, but I must help Bess and George."

"Oh," Audrey persisted, "they can help themselves. I wanted to ask you a few questions about your plans for—"

Nancy looked directly at Audrey Monteith. "I really must ask you to leave," she said firmly. She walked to the door. When they still did not come, she went into the hall. The Monteiths realized their dismissal was complete and finally followed her. As soon as they were outside, Nancy stepped back in and bolted the door.

"Such pests!" she thought, and went into the girls' room.

Her friends were peeling off their costumes, but thinking that the Monteiths might be listening outside, made no comment regarding the couple.

"I brought up a letter for you, Nancy," said George. "It's on the bureau."

Nancy picked it up. "Ned Nickerson!" she told herself. "Good!" Ned, an Emerson College student, had been dating Nancy for many months and had helped her solve several mysteries.

Nancy was delighted with the contents of the letter. Ned had written that he and possibly Burt, who dated George, and Dave, a special friend of Bess's, would come to Camp Merriweather for a couple of days at the beginning of the next week.

"That's just a few days from now!" Nancy thought.

After Bess and George had removed their "Monteith" make-up and were putting on sports-type evening dresses, Nancy peeked into the hall. Their unwelcome callers had disappeared. Coming back, she told the girls what Ned had written.

Instantly Bess, blushing a little, said, "Yum,

that's super news." And George added, "It sure is. But, Nancy, what are you going to do about Rick?"

Nancy pretended to look worried, then said, "Some situations just solve themselves."

Before the girls left the room, George asked, "Nancy, what do you think the Monteiths are up to?"

The girl detective admitted that she was completely puzzled, except that the couple seemed to want to know where she, Bess, and George would be at all times.

"And that gives me an idea," Nancy said. "Why don't we turn the tables and shadow those two for a change?"

"Hypers!" said George. "Why didn't we think of that before? It's a swell idea."

It was decided that as soon as they met Rick, Jack, and Hobe, they would take the boys into their confidence and ask them to do a little spying. Among the three couples they were to keep the Monteiths in sight at all times.

Rick and the other boys were delighted with the plan and Rick remarked, "We thought it was high time you let us know where you've been running off to."

After dinner, while the three couples were talking in the lobby, the Monteiths walked up to them. In their conversation, Nancy and her friends tried to make it appear as if they could hardly wait for the orchestra to start playing and that they would be the last ones to leave the garden when the music stopped. Nancy wondered if it were her imagination or did Ross and Audrey seem to heave a sigh of satisfaction at hearing this?

At intervals during the evening the three couples met and exchanged information. Audrey and Ross were being elusive, darting in and out of the hotel, among the dancers, and even into the woods beyond. It was noticeable that they danced with no one else and even chatted very little with other people.

"I'm sure they're planning something," George remarked with determination.

"Yes, we mustn't lose them," Nancy replied.

A few minutes later as she and Rick were dancing near a path that led from the garden directly to the parking lot, they saw Ross and Audrey suddenly leave the dance floor and disappear. A moment later they emerged onto the path leading to the parking lot.

"There they go!" Nancy told her partner, and together they hurried up the path after the couple.

"I'll go down to the main road and watch which way they turn, while you get your car," Rick offered.

Within a minute Nancy had joined him at the entrance. He jumped in, pointing to the right.

"That's their car down there. They sure left in a hurry."

Nancy put up the top of the convertible to make the automobile less conspicuous, then sped after them. The Monteiths headed directly for the road near which the explosion had taken place that afternoon. They pulled the car to the side of the road and turned off the lights.

As Nancy came closer, Rick said, "There they go across that field."

"They must be heading for the spot where the cave-in was," Nancy remarked.

She found a place a short distance in back of the Monteiths' car where she could park the convertible without its being seen by them should they return. Then she and Rick jumped out and started to follow the couple. Each carried a flashlight but were afraid to turn them on for fear of being discovered. There was moonlight, although it was obscured at times by clouds.

About halfway to the cave-in, Nancy suddenly stopped and whispered, "Someone's behind us."

"And someone's at that cave-in to meet the Monteiths!" said Rick.

The couple wondered if they would be trapped. Rick, wishing to protect Nancy from any harm, felt they should hurry away. But the young sleuth was determined to find out what was going on.

"It's okay with me," said Rick. "You keep looking ahead and I'll try to spot the person in back of us."

"All right," said Nancy. "And we mustn't forget how voices carry. Perhaps we'd better not talk any more."

Silently the two moved ahead until they were very close to the cave-in. Now they could hear two men's voices and knew that the Monteiths had met someone.

By this time the person following Nancy and Rick seemed much closer. Instinctively Nancy and Rick looked around for a place to hide. There was none. Nancy signaled to Rick that their only chance to keep from being seen by the oncoming person was to drop to the ground and remain motionless in the tall grass.

Seconds after they had done this, a tall, well-built stranger stalked by them. Apparently he was not aware of their presence, for he did not stop. He joined the other three at the cave-in and more conversation went on. To her disappointment, Nancy could not distinguish a word.

"I'm sure something sinister is afoot," she thought. "I *must* find out what it is!"

She began to inch forward along the ground to reach a better listening post. Rick followed.

CHAPTER XIII

The Rescue

QUICKLY and silently Nancy and Rick pulled themselves to the edge of the cave-in. Looking into the gaping hole, they saw Ross and Audrey Monteith and the tall stranger making their way down the side. The trio's flashlights were being beamed in all directions. There was no sign of the first man and Nancy and Rick decided he must have left.

"I wonder what those three are looking for," Nancy asked herself.

Ross was tapping his cane here and there. Sometimes he would leave it in one spot for several seconds. Rick's eyes were glued on this maneuver.

"I wish I could get my hands on that cane," he told himself. "It's not an ordinary one. If it doesn't contain a Geiger counter, there's something else inside."

As the trio reached the bottom of the cave-in, they started to talk. Nancy and Rick did their best to hear what was being said but nothing intelligible came to their ears except one phrase:

"We'll have to try another place."

What could this mean? Nancy wondered. Were the trio merely searching for something much as looters might? Or was there more to it? Nancy's mind even toyed with the idea that the Monteiths and their friend had caused the explosion hoping to find something. Having failed to uncover whatever they were looking for, were they going to attempt another dynamiting?

"I'm probably letting my imagination run away with me," Nancy thought. "Anyway, I've told the police my suspicions."

The young sleuth tried to convince herself that she had done her part. But the thought kept recurring to her that perhaps she should get in touch with the authorities again.

"I'll do it the first chance I have," Nancy told herself.

A few minutes later the Monteiths and their friend started up the side of the cave-in. Nancy and Rick tried hard to see the face of the man with the Monteiths, but it was shaded by a large felt hat.

Nancy took hold of her companion's arm and motioned that they had better leave. The two arose and hurried across the field. They had not gone more than three hundred feet when they heard a scream behind them.

"Oh!" Nancy said worriedly. "There must be trouble at the cave-in!"

Despite the fact that she and Rick might be discovered, the couple turned back to be of assistance if necessary. When they reached the torn-up area, the man who had been with the Monteiths was climbing out of the far side. Ross and Audrey Monteith lay face down and almost covered with dirt. They were not moving.

"There's been a landslide! We must save them!" Nancy murmured to Rick.

By this time the companion of the stricken couple had disappeared. Nancy and Rick went down the side of the cave-in, hoping against hope there would not be another landslide. When they safely reached Ross and Audrey, Nancy dug frantically at the dirt around the woman, while Rick clawed to free Ross. Turning them over, their rescuers were delighted to find that the couple were still breathing. But both were unconscious.

"Let's drag Audrey up to the top first," Nancy suggested.

Together she and Rick half pulled, half carried the woman to the top and stretched her on the grass. Then they went back for Ross. As they neared the top of the cave-in with him, dirt began to slide away beneath them and it was only by giving a great leap to the top across the slipping soil that they made it safely.

"Now what?" Rick asked, as he took a deep breath.

Nancy felt the victims' pulses, which were practically normal. Ross and Audrey seemed to have no bruises and she was sure they did not need medical aid.

"We'll wait out of sight until they come to," she said. "Then I think we'd better hurry back to my car. I'd just as soon not have them know we were here."

Rick nodded. "And besides, if they're going on to 'try another place,' I suppose you'd like to follow them."

"I certainly would," Nancy answered.

Fifteen minutes went by before Audrey and Ross Monteith put in an appearance at their car. They showed signs of the shock of their experience and it did not surprise Nancy and Rick to find that the couple drove directly back to Camp Merriweather.

"I guess," said Nancy, "that whatever else the Monteiths had in mind they're not going to carry it out this evening. I'll talk to the police in the morning."

Rick agreed heartily and on the strength of this the two slipped into the hotel by a back entrance and went up a rear stairway so no one would see the grime which covered their faces, arms, and clothes.

"Meet you in twenty minutes," Rick called cheerily, as he started up another flight above the floor on which Nancy's bedroom was located.

The rest of the evening was spent dancing, but in between numbers Nancy and Rick brought Bess, George, and their partners up to date on what had happened. Later the cousins plied Nancy with more detailed questions.

"Ross and Audrey must certainly wonder who rescued them," said George. "Why don't you tell them and then maybe they'll be caught off guard and spill the truth about their plans."

"I'm sure they'll never do it," Nancy told her friends. "And I can see a great advantage in leaving the whole thing mysterious. They must know now that they were followed."

Bess gave a little giggle. "I'd hate to be in their shoes. If I were out to do something shady, and got knocked out and was rescued by a person or persons who didn't tell me about it, boy, would I be worried!"

Nancy grinned. "That's just what I'm counting on. And then there's that man who went off without trying to help the Monteiths. And the man they met first. When one or both of them find out Ross and Audrey were mysteriously rescued, there may be a big powwow among the three or four of them."

"I see what you mean," said George. "The man who left believing the Monteiths were dead may even think he'll have the whole scheme, whatever it is, to himself. When he finds out Ross and Audrey are still in it, the whole bunch may be afraid to go on with any sinister plans."

"Is this what you call a mystery within a mystery?" Bess asked. "You lost me somewhere."

"I suppose it is," Nancy replied. "But someday I hope to find out the answers. Since I've been warned to leave here, it's just possible all this has something to do with the clue in the old stagecoach. If the Monteiths and their confederates give up, it may make things easier for us."

Nancy then said she was going to call on Mrs. Pauling the next morning. "I'll ask her if she'd be willing to pay the Zuckers for the old Langstreet stagecoach if it's found on their property. Then at least it could be restored."

The three girls hurried into bed but were up early and ready for the trip next morning. Nancy talked to the police, then started off for Mrs. Pauling's home.

She was just finishing her breakfast in the modern, attractively decorated dining room, and invited them to share pieces of homemade toasted cinnamon bread and cocoa with her. Its aroma was so delightful the girls could not refuse and sat down with her.

"How is the stagecoach mystery coming?" Mrs. Pauling asked, smiling.

"We may have a little problem," Nancy replied, then added, "If the old stagecoach is found on the Zucker property, the young couple may feel they should be reimbursed if it is taken away."

"I'll be very happy to take care of that," Mrs. Pauling said quickly. "And I'll do even more. I'll pay for having it restored and taken to Bridgeford." She sighed, then added, "How I wish I had money enough to build a new school for the community! But that would be beyond my means."

"It's wonderful to have you help the restoration," Nancy remarked. She said the girls were going to the Zucker farm at once, and if permitted, would start digging operations to hunt for the old vehicle.

"I wish you luck—much luck," Mrs. Pauling said as she waved farewell to them from the front door a little while later.

When Nancy, Bess, and George reached the Zucker farm, they were warmly greeted by Marjory and Morton. The couple were delighted to learn that Mrs. Pauling would be willing to pay for the old stagecoach if it were found on the property.

"Do you want to start searching right away?" Morton asked.

"Yes, indeed," Nancy answered. "I hope that you have lots of digging tools."

"That's one thing I do have." Morton laughed. He went to the barn and brought a spade, a shovel, and a pickax. Marjory produced a large garden trowel.

"The baby's asleep now," she said, "so I can help you. I'll put Jimmy in his play pen and wheel him to wherever we're going."

A lengthy discussion took place as to the most likely spot in which Mr. Langstreet might have buried the stagecoach. The ground beneath the original buildings was discarded by Nancy, who felt he would have been afraid that the structures might be razed and the old vehicle found.

"I'm sure it was not Mr. Langstreet's intention at first that anyone was ever to know where it was. It was only years later, just before his death, that he decided to tell."

Morton and Marjory had another theory. "All the plowed fields on this farm have been gone over many times," Morton remarked. "It seems to me that the old stagecoach would have been found long before this if it had been buried in one of the fields."

The others agreed and Marjory said, "That only leaves the woods. The question, now, is which woods?"

Morton pointed out that all of them were a bit swampy with the exception of a wooded knoll about a thousand feet from the house. "I vote that we start digging there," he suggested.

"Let's go!" said George, starting across the field with a spade swung over her shoulder.

Nancy helped Mrs. Zucker half carry, half roll the baby's play pen across the rough ground. They parked the infant in the shade of one of the trees, then all started digging with a will.

Dirt piled up in mounds, as the diggers went from one spot to another. Presently they stood under a dead tree next to the one where the baby was asleep.

Digging started here with great energy. Suddenly they heard a cracking sound and Bess screamed:

"George, run!"

CHAPTER XIV

A Hopeful Discovery

WITHOUT asking the reason, George dropped her spade and ran some distance away. A moment later a large limb of the dead tree crashed to the ground.

Nancy, working on the other side of the old tree, had looked up at Bess's cry and realized what was going to happen. She feared that the dead wood might splinter and one or more pieces hit the baby!

Jumping to the play pen, she wheeled it out of the way. She too was just in time. Chunks of wood were hurled through the air. Some of them landed exactly where the play pen had stood!

"Oh, Nancy," Mrs. Zucker cried out, "you kept my baby from being hurt!" She hugged Nancy, then picked up the infant, who had been jolted awake by this time and had begun to cry. "I—I think I'll go back to the house," the young mother added.

In the meantime George's heartbeat had returned to normal. She thanked her cousin for the warning, then grinned ruefully. "I'd have had a pretty bad bump if that old limb had ever hit me!"

Morton Zucker said he felt responsible for the whole thing. He had promised himself many times to take down the dead tree but had never seemed to have time.

"But you can bet it's going to come down fast now," he said with determination.

The diggers decided to go on with their work but to have one of them as a lookout at all times.

"I'll watch first," Bess offered, and kept her eyes on the rotted limbs of the old tree.

Nancy, George, and Morton dug furiously. Several times they hit roots. At these moments the searchers hoped they had struck a piece of the old stagecoach or at least a container holding some of its parts. But they had no luck and moved on to another location.

At noontime Bess spoke up. "Let's take a rest. I forgot to tell you girls I brought some lunch for us. I had the camp chef pack it."

She went for the package and the three girls sat down in the shade of the knoll to eat roast-beef sandwiches, tomatoes, and cake. Morton, upon learning they had brought their own food, went to the house to get his lunch. In an hour he was back and the work continued.

Time after time fragments of tools and hardware were dug up, but none of them belonged to an old stagecoach. Bess and George became weary of their task. They were just about to suggest quitting, when Morton, who had been quiet for several minutes, called out from a distance:

"Maybe this is what you're looking for!"

The three girls rushed to his side, just as he lifted up an old wheel.

"We've found it!" Bess shrieked excitedly.

The whole group dug furiously in the vicinity. Presently they unearthed a matching wheel, then a third, finally a fourth. All were in bad condition and two would fall apart if lifted up.

"Now where shall we dig?" George asked.

Morton said he thought one person's guess was as good as another. "Why don't we dig all the way around these wheels?" he suggested.

They did this and within a few minutes uncovered some rotted leather straps.

"Oh, this is so thrilling!" Bess exclaimed, putting her full weight onto the spade she was using. "I've hit something!"

Nancy helped her dig and presently they uncovered a long board. Further digging revealed rusty hinges once attached to the plank. Then came another board evidently originally hinged to the other, but now rotted apart.

"*Maybe this is what you're looking for!*"

At almost the same time Morton uncovered a series of long boards. He frowned, then said regretfully, "These could not have belonged to a stagecoach. This was just a farm wagon. It's my guess the wagon was wrecked at this spot or dragged here and time covered it with earth."

Bess seemed more disappointed than the others. She had felt so sure the mystery was about to be solved, the frustrated girl was almost in tears.

"This is just awful!" she said, flopping to the ground. "All this work and nothing but a busted old wagon!"

"And it's been here a long time, I'll bet," said George. "I wonder if it belonged to Abner Langstreet."

Nancy thought it might have. "If he took his old stagecoach apart and carried the pieces away, he would have needed some kind of vehicle to cart it in."

Bess was inconsolable. "If we keep on digging, we may find the bones of the horses to this wagon," she said. "I vote we quit right now. Anyway, George and I promised to play tennis late this afternoon."

Morton said that he too would have to stop work and do the evening farm chores. "But I shan't stop digging entirely," he promised Nancy. "You have my curiosity aroused. If that old stagecoach is buried on this farm, I'll find it!"

Nancy was very weary herself from the arduous

work and did not argue about stopping. They all trudged back to the farmhouse where Mrs. Zucker insisted they have glasses of cold milk. The girls washed their faces and hands and then sat down in the living room to cool off.

"I had callers while you were at work," said Marjory Zucker.

"Callers?" Nancy repeated.

"Yes, a man and a woman about thirty years old. They asked if this was the Robert Smith farm. Of course I told them no."

"Did you give them your name?" Nancy asked.

"Yes."

Marjory went on to say that the couple had stood near their car and watched the digging operation at the knoll. The man had asked what was going on.

"You didn't tell them?" Nancy asked worriedly.

"Oh, no," Marjory replied. "I said farmers are always digging."

"Good for you!" George spoke up.

Nancy asked for descriptions of the couple and the car. Upon hearing them, she looked at Bess and George. There was no question in any of their minds. The callers had been Audrey and Ross Monteith!

"Do you know the people who were here?" Marjory asked. "I had an idea they might have suspected it was you at the knoll, Nancy, because they asked who owned your car. When I ignored the question, they looked at each other as if they knew."

"We know them all right," said Nancy. "They're staying at the same lodge where we are. We find them—well, a little too interested in our affairs!"

"I see," Marjory answered with an understanding smile.

The three girls said good-by, adding that they might return soon. As they drove off toward the main road, Bess wore a worried frown. "I don't like it at all that Audrey and Ross Monteith were here!"

"I don't either," Nancy agreed.

CHAPTER XV

Startling News

"When we get home," said George, her jaw set firmly, "I'm going to have it out with Ross and Audrey Monteith! They're a pain, and besides, I can't take being followed any longer."

Nancy tried to dissuade her friend from carrying out her threat. "It may only drive Ross and Audrey into hiding and then they'll have the advantage over us. They'll know where we are, but we won't know where they are."

"All right," George finally conceded. "But it certainly burns me up having them act the way they do."

After the girls had put the car in the parking lot, they walked up to the front of Camp Merriweather lodge. Rick Larrabee and his friends arose from a nearby bench to greet them. All three looked very sober.

"I'm glad you came," said Rick. "We have news for you."

Before he could go on, Hobe White burst forth with, "The Monteiths have checked out!"

"What!" the three girls exclaimed together.

Rick explained that he and the other fellows had decided to do some sleuthing. "We thought we'd surprise you girls," he said. "To our amazement, we learned that the Monteiths had packed their bags and left Merriweather before breakfast."

"Where did they go?" Nancy asked quickly.

Rick shrugged. "I asked the clerk if he knew where. All he could tell me was that the Monteiths had asked that their mail be forwarded to a post-office box in New York City."

"And that sounds zany to me," said Hobe. "The Monteiths have been here for two weeks. The clerk says they haven't received one piece of mail."

"That does look suspicious," Nancy agreed. "It wouldn't surprise me if the Monteiths have moved to another hotel in this area, or more likely to a private home and perhaps under an assumed name."

"What about their car license?" Bess asked. "Wouldn't that give them away?"

Nancy smiled and said, "When I phoned the police this morning, they told me the car which the Monteiths are driving is registered in the name of Frank Templer."

"So they are using an assumed name!" George cried out. "I knew they were phonies from the start."

"Not so fast," said Nancy. "The Monteiths might have borrowed the car from Mr. Frank Templer."

"Or," Rick spoke up, "Ross's real name may be Frank Templer," and Nancy nodded.

Rick now told the girls his other bit of news. "We fellows are mighty sorry, but we must leave camp right away."

"Now?" asked Bess, genuinely sorry to hear this. Nancy and George were too.

"I'm afraid so," Rick answered. "A little while ago I had word that my father is very ill. Mother wants me to come home. I told Hobe it wasn't necessary for him to drive me there—that I'd take the train."

"But I insisted," said Hobe. "We're leaving in a little while. I hope you girls get your mystery solved. Lots of luck!"

Nancy thanked Rick for all the help he had given her. She and the other girls said they hoped Mr. Larrabee would have a speedy recovery.

Hobe's car was parked not far from the hotel entrance. The whole group now walked over to it and the boys climbed aboard. Good-bys were said and the girls waved as the car went down the driveway and out the entrance gate.

"They're three nice fellows," George remarked, as the girls went into the lodge and took the elevator to their rooms.

Nancy and Bess agreed and Bess added, "This mystery is going to get dangerous—I just have a hunch. We need some boys to help us. I'm glad Ned and Burt and Dave are coming."

Nancy laughed. "Danger or no danger," she said, "I'm glad they're coming too."

After she had showered and dressed, the young sleuth sat in deep thought for some time. What should she do next? Suddenly her puzzled mood changed. "I know what I'll do," she told herself. "I'll call Dad. He'll give me some good advice."

It had been arranged at home that while Nancy was on vacation with Bess and George, her father would live at his club. Their housekeeper, Hannah Gruen, was going to visit relatives. Mrs. Gruen had lived with the Drews for many years and had helped to rear Nancy, whose mother had passed away when Nancy was only three years old.

Nancy stuck her head into the adjoining room and told the girls she was going downstairs to a private phone booth and put in a long-distance call to her father. Soon she had the club on the wire and asked for Mr. Drew. Hoping fervently that he would be there, Nancy held the receiver and tapped one foot in nervous anticipation.

A few moments later she was delighted to hear a deep-sounding voice say, "Hello, Nancy dear!"

"Dad!" his daughter cried happily. "I'm so glad you were in. Dad, I'm full of problems and I need your advice."

Carson Drew chuckled. "Shall I have my dinner sent here and eat it while you talk?" he teased. "But seriously, tell me first how you are and then I'll listen to your problems. I'm sure they involve some mystery."

Nancy said she was feeling fine, then launched into the story of the stagecoach mystery and the various setbacks she had had.

"Well, you certainly have been busy," Mr. Drew remarked, as she finished. "And the mystery sounds like a most intriguing one. Now what is it exactly you want me to help you with?"

"Tell me first, am I on the right track in the way I've gone about this?" the young sleuth asked.

"I'd say you are," the lawyer replied. "And I think your surmises so far have probably been correct. So go on with your digging operations. But if I were you, before I did any more of it, I'd try to find out who the former owners or tenants of the Zucker property were. Perhaps they can give you some clue as to where the stagecoach might have been buried."

"Dad," said Nancy, feeling a new surge of enthusiasm, "I knew you'd tell me exactly the right thing to do. I'll ask the Zuckers, and if they don't know, I'll go to the courthouse and look at the records."

"I wish I could come up there and help you," said Mr. Drew, "but I'm deep in problems of my own here on a case. I must own up, though, I'm getting lonesome. Don't let that case of yours take too long to solve!"

"Dad, I miss you very much too," said Nancy. "I'll speed things up and get home as fast as I can."

When Nancy met Bess and George for dinner, both cousins remarked that Nancy seemed very refreshed and gay. Chuckling, she told them why. "Tomorrow morning we'll go to see the Zuckers. I have a strange feeling that I've sort of turned the corner in this mystery."

"Thank goodness," said Bess. "Nancy, I was beginning to worry about you."

Fortunately, the Zuckers had a complete list of the former owners of the farm, starting with the man from whom Abner Langstreet had rented it.

"But only two of these people are alive now," Morton said. "One is elderly Mr. Hanson who lives in a government home for war veterans outside Francisville. The other is Mrs. Stryker, who is much younger. She's the widow of the man who owned this place just before we bought it. He was killed on that hill"—she pointed—"when a tractor overturned on him."

"How dreadful!" Bess murmured.

Nancy said the girls would go immediately to interview these people and then perhaps come back to do some digging. Morton Zucker told them he had done a little more work up near the knoll the evening before but had found nothing.

"See you later," Nancy called, as she started the car's motor.

She drove directly to the veterans' home. Mr. Hanson, old and feeble, was delighted to learn he had callers. Once he started to talk, there was no stopping him. It soon became evident that while he could recall vividly events which had happened a long time ago, he was very hazy about the days when he had lived on the farm.

"I'm not learning anything about the stage-coach," Nancy thought.

Finally she gave up, arose, and said the girls must leave. Mr. Hanson tried his best to keep them from going as he said he had much more to tell. But they felt sure he had never unearthed anything on the farm property.

"We've enjoyed talking with you very much," said Nancy politely.

The girls left and went directly to Mrs. Stryker's home in Francisville. Nancy apologized for the intrusion and the necessity of having to talk about the woman's late husband. A tear rolled down Mrs. Stryker's face, but she said it was all right, then asked how she could help the girls.

To Nancy's questions the woman replied that she felt sure nothing large was buried on any part of the property, except perhaps on the wooded knoll, the only unplowed area on the farm.

"My dear husband was an excellent farmer," she said. "He plowed deep and kept every inch of the soil under fine cultivation. If he had ever come across anything worth mentioning, I know he would have told me."

"Then I'm probably entirely wrong in my guess that something of value may be on the property," said Nancy.

She thanked Mrs. Stryker for giving them the information she had and was about to leave when the woman said, "You're the second person within twenty-four hours to come inquiring about the Zucker property."

Nancy stopped short in amazement. "Really?" she said. "Would you mind telling me who the other person was?"

"It was a man," Mrs. Stryker answered. "He said his name was Frank Templer."

Nancy and her friends were startled. Quickly Nancy asked for a description of Frank Templer. The minute she and Bess and George heard it they knew the person was Ross Monteith!

"Did Mr.—er—Templer say where he was staying?" Nancy inquired eagerly.

"Well not exactly," said Mrs. Stryker, "but I

gathered it was somewhere in this area. Do you know Mr. Templer?"

"I think so," said Nancy, "only I know him by another name. That's why I'm so interested to find out about him."

"Something else he said may help you," Mrs. Stryker went on. "Mr. Templer said that he was a member of the family which originally owned the Zucker place. He was trying to find something valuable which had been buried years ago."

"Did he mention the name of the family?" Nancy queried.

"Yes, he did," the woman replied. "He said it was Langstreet."

"I see," said Nancy. "Thank you very much, Mrs. Stryker. Please forgive me for having bothered you, but it may turn out that you will have helped several people."

"I'm always glad to help anyone," said Mrs. Stryker.

The girls went out to the convertible. As soon as they were seated in it, George asked Nancy what she thought of this latest bit of information.

"It's terrific!" the young sleuth said. "Apparently Mr. Templer doesn't know that Abner Langstreet never owned the Zucker farm, but only rented it!"

"That's right," said George. "So Ross *isn't* a descendant. He's only pretending to be so he can claim any fortune found on the place."

"Sounds like him," Bess remarked, and added, "Where are you going now, Nancy?"

"To Mrs. Strook's and ask her about the Langstreet family tree."

The elderly woman was amazed at Nancy's information. "I never heard of anyone in our family named Monteith or Templer either."

Nancy suggested that it was possible Mr. Abner Langstreet had married after disappearing from Francisville.

"Then why didn't any relatives show up at the time of his death?" the elderly woman argued.

"That's exactly what I'm wondering," Nancy said.

CHAPTER XVI

A Harrowing Appointment

ON THE way back to Camp Merriweather, Bess acknowledged her fear that the Monteiths, if balked too far, might try to harm the girls.

"You're right," said George. "The sooner we find that two-faced couple the better!"

Bess looked at her cousin. "And just how are we going to do that with no clues?"

George did not reply, but Nancy said, "What seems important to me is to have courthouse, church, and cemetery records searched to find out if Abner Langstreet did marry and have any children. When we get back to the lodge, I think I'll call Dad and ask him to do this for me."

Nancy's father thought this was a good idea and said he would arrange for someone in the neighborhood of Francisville to make the search. "I'll call you back, Nancy," he promised.

Within fifteen minutes he phoned that a young

lawyer in Francisville by the name of Art Warner would take the case.

"I've asked him to let you know what he learns, Nancy," Mr. Drew told her.

"Dad," she said, "if it's true that Ross Monteith is a direct descendant of Abner Langstreet, would the old stagecoach belong to him?"

"Perhaps," her father replied. "It would depend upon what was put into the deed of sale of the property where the old vehicle is found. Art Warner will get all these facts for you."

"All right, Dad, and thanks so much."

Nancy joined her friends. Upon hearing the results of the conversation with Mr. Drew, Bess remarked, "I guess we can't do much until we hear from this Art Warner. It will give us a good chance to have some fun."

She said there was to be a water ballet in a few nights. Tryouts were being held now.

"Let's go and see how we rate," she suggested.

Nancy was torn between a desire to concede to Bess's wish and to save all her time for solving the mystery. She realized that both Bess and George had given up a lot of fun at the lodge in order to help her. She must do her part by acceding to their wishes.

"All right," she said, smiling. "Let's put on our bathing suits and try out right now."

The three girls changed, then went downstairs. A large crowd had gathered at the pool to watch.

One after another of the girl campers was asked to try out her skill swimming to a waltz tune, then to a lively number.

When it came time for Nancy, Bess, and George to try out, Bess asked the social director, who was running the affair, if they might swim together.

"Yes. Go ahead."

The girls dived into the deep end of the pool and gracefully "waltzed" across the water. At one point they were asked to turn on their backs and swim in time to the music. When they finally reached the far edge of the pool, the music suddenly changed to a fast number. Impishly George said to her friends:

"Let's put on a comedy act."

"Okay," Nancy and Bess agreed. "You lead us, George."

They dived beneath one another, as if barely missing a crash, reared up out of the water, made comical faces, and disappeared beneath the surface all in perfect rhythm to the music. The crowd along the shore clapped and shouted.

"Pretty neat," called out a red-haired boy.

When the names of the finalists were read, there was no question but that the three girls from River Heights were among those chosen for the water ballet.

"Will you please come see the director about costumes?" the swimming instructor requested. He had been the final judge.

As Nancy and her chums stood talking with the social director, a bellhop came to tell Nancy she was wanted on the telephone. She hurried off, wondering who might be calling—her father, Ned Nickerson, Hannah Gruen—

Nancy found herself completely thunderstruck when the voice at the other end of the line said, "Nancy, this is Audrey Monteith. How are you?"

The young sleuth said she was fine. With frigid politeness she asked, "How are you and Ross? And why did you leave Merriweather in such a hurry?"

"Oh, we feel much better," Audrey replied. "We couldn't stand the camp another minute. Such food! We felt positively ill most of the time."

"Where are you staying now?" Nancy inquired.

"Oh, at a very fashionable, exclusive resort," Audrey answered, but did not give the name of the place. Quickly she went on, "Nancy, you're just the person to help Ross and me. We've stumbled onto a little mystery we'd like you to solve."

"I'm very busy," Nancy said. "There wouldn't be time for me to—"

"Why, I'm surprised," said Audrey. "I didn't think you ever turned down a chance to solve a mystery. And this is a pretty keen one."

"What is it?" Nancy asked.

Audrey Monteith said it concerned a deserted farmhouse located only half a mile out of Francisville. "It's on Tulip Road which runs off Main Street. It wouldn't take you long, I'm sure. Please come meet us day after tomorrow. Later, Ross and I will take you to lunch in town."

Nancy hesitated. Her first hunch was that this was some kind of a trap and she did not propose to be caught in it.

But she argued with herself, "If I don't go, I may be cheating myself and the police out of picking up a clue about the Monteiths' recent actions. This deserted farmhouse they're talking about might have something to do with the old stagecoach!"

"All right, I'll meet you Monday morning," Nancy promised.

"Let's make it eleven thirty," Audrey said.

Nancy agreed, then asked, "Where can I get in touch with you, if I find it necessary to change the date?"

Audrey did not answer the question directly. She said, "If you don't show up by twelve o'clock I'll call you at the lodge." She hung up.

Later on, when Nancy was alone with Bess and George, she told them about the phone call. The cousins were worried and advised caution. Bess added, "Surely you're not going alone?"

Nancy laughed. "Not unless you two walk out on me," she said.

George made a face at Nancy. "You know perfectly well we'd never do that."

Nancy said she would notify the police of the appointment. While talking with the chief, she learned that the department had not been able to find the suspicious couple.

"I'll have a man or two hidden near that farmhouse to watch proceedings," the chief said. "Then later they can follow the Monteiths."

Late Monday morning the girls set off. The deserted farmhouse proved to be easy to find. Nancy turned into the lane and parked near the dilapidated weather-beaten building. As the girls stepped out of the convertible, she said:

"Just in case the Monteiths are planning to trick us, let's watch all directions at once. We can sit down here on the walk with our backs to one another."

"Suits me," George agreed. "Say, I wonder where the police are. They're certainly well hidden."

In five minutes it was eleven thirty, but the Monteiths had not arrived. After ten minutes had gone by, George spoke up, "I'm afraid there is some trick to this."

"Yes," said Bess, "I'm beginning to think the Monteiths just wanted to be sure of knowing where you were, Nancy. They're working some scheme miles from here—maybe at the Zucker farm."

Nancy frowned. At ten minutes to twelve she

felt inclined to agree with her friends. "I'll wait until twelve and then we'll leave," she said disgustedly.

The words were hardly out of her mouth when the earth began to shake. "Another explosion!" George cried.

As the girls jumped to their feet, the dilapidated farmhouse suddenly began to fall apart! They fled in terror. Just in time they got beyond the crashing structure.

"Your car, Nancy!" George exclaimed.

The convertible was struck by pieces of flying wood and broken glass. A few bricks from the chimney had landed in the rear seat. But there was no major damage.

"Thank goodness we're all right," said Nancy.

After the girls collected their wits, they went over and began to clean out the car. Bess found a polishing cloth and set to work shining up the scratched and nicked spots.

"I wonder what happened to the police," George said. "Seems to me they'd come out of hiding now."

Bess clapped a hand to her cheek. "Oh, you don't suppose they were inside the building!" she cried in horror.

"No," said Nancy. "They were to hide nearby. It's my guess that since they can see we're all right, they won't bother to let us know where they are.

I think they'll stay here a long time in case the Monteiths show up. It's possible Ross and Audrey won't come until after we girls have left."

The three friends began to discuss the explosion. It had been very similar to the previous one and there was no doubt in their minds but that the same people had perpetrated both of them.

"Do you think the Monteiths knew it was going to happen?" Bess asked. "And they're mean enough to have sent us here, hoping we'd be injured?"

"I certainly wouldn't put it past them," George answered.

Even Nancy felt that this guess on Bess's part might well be true. Then she tried to shake off the thought. "Perhaps the Monteiths didn't keep the date because they were tipped off about the police. We'll wait a little longer."

But though the girls waited until twelve thirty, Ross and Audrey did not drive up. Even then Nancy said that she might hear from them again by telephone. George, however, was skeptical that this would ever happen.

The girls left and headed for the center of town. "I want to talk to Art Warner and see what he may have learned about Abner Langstreet," said Nancy.

Bess and George waited in the car, while Nancy went to see the young lawyer. To her astonishment, Judd Hillary sat in the reception room. He glanced at Nancy malevolently. "You came to see Mr. Warner? Well, you can't do it, Nancy Drew! I got a previous appointment. And it'll take several hours!"

CHAPTER XVII

Burglars!

AT A desk in the corner of Art Warner's reception room sat an attractive, middle-aged woman. Hearing Judd Hillary's outburst, she looked up quickly and frowned at the man. She smiled at Nancy and gave her a look as if to notify the girl she had come to a sudden decision.

"Miss Drew," she said, "Mr. Warner will see you at once."

Judd Hillary fell back in his chair as if he had been struck. A dark, angry flush spread over his face as the secretary opened the door to the lawyer's private office and ushered Nancy in. As the door closed behind the young sleuth, she could hear loud complaints from Hillary.

"Hello," said a young man who had arisen from his desk to greet her. He was tall, wore horn-rimmed glasses, and had an infectious smile.

"I'm Nancy Drew," his caller whispered. "You

probably heard what happened outside. Your secretary was a dear to let me come in."

Art Warner gave Nancy a big wink, then said in a low voice, "I told Miss Blake you might drop in sometime. She played her part well." The young lawyer laughed. "Apparently you and Mr. Hillary are acquainted but are not the best of friends."

"Far from it," Nancy replied.

Art Warner pulled a chair close to his own, so that the conversation to follow would not be heard in the outside room.

"My dad probably told you something about the mystery," the young sleuth began, "but I doubt that he told you of certain suspicions of mine regarding Judd Hillary. Since he's a client of yours, perhaps I shouldn't say any more."

Art Warner smiled. "He hasn't become a client yet, so feel free to tell me anything you wish to. The more I know, the better position I'll be in to help you."

"All right," said Nancy. "I'll start at the beginning."

She told about the Monteiths' strange actions, of their presence at the cave-in, and of the date they had made and failed to keep just before the second explosion. Nancy went on to reveal the story about the hijackers of the stagecoach and her feeling that Judd Hillary was the man in the woods who had whistled to warn them.

Art Warner frowned. "I had no idea this was such a complicated mystery," he remarked.

The lawyer stared out the window a full minute before speaking again. "I'm glad you've told me all this," he said finally. "I'm eager to learn whether or not what Judd Hillary is waiting to say will have anything to do with your mystery."

Nancy nodded and now asked Art Warner if he had had a chance yet to find out if Abner Langstreet had ever married.

"I was telephoning all morning about the case," the lawyer answered. "Of course I haven't covered every possibility. But it looks as if Langstreet remained a bachelor. At least this much is certain: If he ever married, he went some distance away from Francisville to have the ceremony performed. And if he did have a wife who died before he did, she's not buried in any cemetery in this locale."

The lawyer added that he had investigated church registers and town-hall records where a few vital statistics were kept at that time. "None of them reveal his having married anyone, and from what Mrs. Strook was told by her family, it's pretty certain he never did."

"If this is true," said Nancy, "then it makes Ross Monteith, or Frank Templer, an impostor."

"It sure does," Art Warner agreed.

Nancy next queried him on what he knew about the explosion. Mr. Warner said it was thought to have taken place under the Francisville end of one of the housing developments.

"That's not far from where we girls were," Nancy told him. "It seems almost certain that the Monteiths got me there on purpose."

Art Warner asked Nancy if she thought there was any connection between Judd Hillary and the Monteiths.

"There might be," she said. "The three of them have acted strangely toward me, and shown a lot of curiosity about what I've been doing. I could almost believe the Monteiths told Hillary I was looking for the old stagecoach."

"I'll try adroitly to find out what I can for you," the young lawyer promised.

Nancy knew that he was eager to have the interview with Judd Hillary, so she arose and said good-by.

"I'll keep you informed," Mr. Warner promised.

When Nancy reached the reception room, she gave Miss Blake a big smile. The young sleuth merely nodded to Judd Hillary, then went downstairs and joined Bess and George.

When she told them about her unpleasant experience in the outer office, Bess asked, "What do you suppose Judd Hillary came there for?"

Nancy shrugged. "I can't guess, but unless it's something very confidential, I think Art Warner will let me know about it."

The girls returned to the lodge for a late lunch. No telephone message had been received from the Monteiths and Nancy was sure now that she had been tricked into going to the dilapidated farmhouse for one of two reasons: either to be deliberately harmed, or else to be kept from doing any sleuthing on the stagecoach mystery at that particular time.

"Does this mean," Nancy asked herself, "that the Monteiths are afraid I'm getting too near the truth and might have trailed the dynamiters?"

Just as the girls finished eating, Nancy received a phone call from Art Warner. He said that Judd Hillary's reason for coming to him was that he wanted to sell a certain piece of property. It did not have a clear title and he was asking the lawyer to make a new search.

"You didn't learn anything about a possible connection of his with the mystery?" Nancy asked eagerly.

"I'm afraid not," Art Warner replied. "As a matter of fact, Judd Hillary seemed very ill at ease and anxious to get away as quickly as possible. If he's guilty of anything underhanded, I believe he thinks you might have told me of your suspicions."

Nancy was disappointed, but she made no comment. She thanked Mr. Warner for calling her and asked him to let her know any further developments.

As Nancy rejoined her friends, they told her a practice period was scheduled for the water ballet in one hour. "We're to be at the pool for a workout," said Bess.

When the three girls arrived there, the swimming instructor and the social director asked them if they would perform their comedy act for the final show the same way they had done it in the tryouts. Nancy and her friends agreed, but said they felt they should vary it a little, since a good many people had seen it before.

There were few onlookers at the pool now and the girls decided it would be an ideal time to practice. Bess asked what kind of costumes they should wear for the event.

George grinned. "We act like three clowns, so I think clown-type bathing suits would be appropriate."

Bess demurred. "I don't mind the suit," she said, "but what about our hair and faces? I don't want to wear a frizzy wig and one of those great big red noses like clowns do."

George's grin widened as she said teasingly, "Of course you wouldn't, especially in front of a certain boy named Dave."

Bess noticed that George was looking past her toward the lodge. The next moment she waved. Bess turned quickly to see Ned Nickerson, Burt Eddleton, and Dave Evans! The three boys, all with deep suntans and crew cuts, hurried over.

"Hi, everybody!" said the boys and girls almost simultaneously.

Ned grinned. "I guess we're just in time to see three beautiful mermaids. Go ahead and do your stuff."

"Mermaids?" Nancy answered with a twinkle in her eyes. "We're just a trio of clowns."

"What do you mean?" Dave demanded, mystified.

Nancy refused to explain and none of the boys could learn the answer from either Bess or George. "You'll know in a few days," George said.

Nancy told them about the water ballet and that the girls must practice for it. "But by the time you fellows unpack and get into your bathing trunks, we'll be ready to take a swim with you."

"Neat," said Burt, and the three boys hurried off.

After the promised swim was over, the six young people sat down at a large table beside the pool. As they sipped lemonade and munched pretzels and nuts which the camp always served at this hour, Nancy brought the boys up to date on the mystery.

Ned whistled in amazement. "It's sure a dilly. Sounds as if it has about six parts to it."

Burt laughed. "Maybe each of us should take one part. We'll do it in shifts. One hour on, and two hours off—in couples, of course."

"That's a great idea," Nancy conceded. "But I think that before starting, you boys should become acquainted with the people and places involved in the mystery. We still have time this afternoon to go to the deserted village at Bridgeford. Then we could stop at Mrs. Strook's. What say?"

"Good enough," Ned agreed. "Let's get dressed and go right away." A short time later they all set off.

The boys were intrigued by the restoration of the old-time village. John O'Brien was there and Nancy introduced her friends to the trucker. They discussed the old stagecoach and the hijacking, then the young people left.

When they reached Mrs. Strook's home a little while later, Nancy rang the front doorbell. There was no answer.

"Mrs. Strook must be out," the young sleuth commented, "but it's strange that she would leave her front door open. I want you boys to see this quaint house. I'm sure Mrs. Strook wouldn't mind. Let's go in and look around."

She led the way into the living room and then gasped. The place had been ransacked! The desk drawers were open, with papers scattered over the floor. Sofa cushions had been thrown helterskelter, and books tossed from wall shelves.

"Oh, how dreadful!" Bess cried out.

Nancy's next thought was for Mrs. Strook's

safety. Had the burglars harmed her? The young sleuth began running through the various rooms of the first floor to see if the woman were there.

"Oh!" she exclaimed suddenly.

Nancy had just entered a first-floor bedroom. On the bed lay the elderly Mrs. Strook, bound and gagged!

CHAPTER XVIII

Whirring Cameras

NANCY's friends crowded into Mrs. Strook's bedroom. "Oh!" Bess exclaimed. "Has she been hurt?"

"I think not," Nancy replied.

Before she untied the knots with which Mrs. Strook had been firmly bound and gagged, she said to Ned and the other boys, "Aren't these nautical knots?"

"They sure are," Ned answered emphatically. "Some sailor or ex-sailor tied Mrs. Strook up with clove hitches."

He helped Nancy release the elderly woman from her bonds. Gently Nancy advised Mrs. Strook not to sit up. "Just take it easy and tell us what you can," she said.

"I'll get you some hot tea," Bess offered, and hurried to the kitchen.

Nancy introduced Ned, Burt, and Dave. The stricken woman nodded to them but seemed too shocked to reply. But after she had sipped the tea which Bess brought, Mrs. Strook insisted upon getting up and sitting in a chair. Then she began her story.

"It was awful—just awful," she said. "Two men came to the door and the moment I opened it, they rushed in. One of them said 'We're not goin' to fool around. We want a quick answer. What was Langstreet's secret?' "

"How in the world did they find that out?" George interposed.

"I have no idea," the elderly woman answered. "When I told them I didn't know, they said they'd find out themselves. That's when they tied me up and gagged me so I couldn't yell. They searched this house thoroughly, I'm sure, from the racket I heard. Oh, I hate to think of going outside this room and looking!"

"Please don't do it," said Nancy. "We'd offer to clean things up for you, but the police never want anything disturbed. I must call them. But first, tell me what the men looked like."

Mrs. Strook said she did not know. Both wore masks and hats pulled down so far over their foreheads that she could not tell the color of their hair.

"By any chance, did one have a scar on his wrist?" Nancy asked.

"I don't know that, either. Both men wore long gloves."

"But we do have one possible clue," Nancy said. "The nautical knots. I think I can give the police a good tip as to who the thugs might have been."

Mrs. Strook became very pale again, and Nancy insisted upon her lying on the bed. The boys left the room and went to look around for any other clues to the intruders.

"Perhaps you should go to the hospital, Mrs. Strook," Bess spoke up. "At least until the mess here is straightened out."

The woman shook her head. "I don't feel bad enough to go to the hospital," she insisted. "A little rest will fix me up, I'm sure. Anyway, I want to be here to answer any questions the police may have."

Nancy had felt Bess's suggestion a good one but could not go against the woman's wishes. Now she said, "Perhaps you have some friend or neighbor who will be able to stay with you for a few days?"

Mrs. Strook said she would like this. She gave Nancy a list of names to call. The third one on it, a Mrs. Grover, said she would be happy to help.

Nancy now phoned police headquarters and told her story to Sergeant Hurley. He promised to send a man to Mrs. Strook's as soon as possible. At present most of the force was investigating the explosion.

It was fully an hour before two officers arrived. They were the sergeant himself and Detective Takman.

Mrs. Strook repeated her story, then Nancy told of her suspicion as to who the two thugs might have been.

"This is amazing," Sergeant Hurley remarked. "Those hijackers have eluded the police so far." The officer smiled at Nancy. "You wouldn't have any idea where they are right now, would you, Miss Drew?"

"I wish I did," she answered. "I'd like to ask them a few questions myself!"

During most of this conversation, only Nancy and the officers had been in the room with Mrs. Strook. Bess and George had joined the boys outdoors. They found that Ned had traced the intruders' footprints around the house and through a hedge to the next property. Burt had gone into the kitchen for some string and had "roped" off the footprints.

"Aren't you boys clever!" Bess praised them. "Any more clues?"

"Yes," Dave spoke up. "I'll show you one."

At that moment Nancy came from the house with the police officers. When the roped-off area was pointed out to them, Sergeant Hurley said, "Are all of you detectives?"

"The only real detective among us is Nancy

Drew, but we all go to her training school," Burt Eddleton spoke up with a grin.

"Well, I can see that she teaches good courses," the officer said. "Did you find out anything else, young man?"

Dave led them to a spot near the hedge. A man's dark-brown glove lay on the ground. "Mrs. Strook said the thugs wore gloves. Perhaps this is one of them."

From his pocket Detective Takman took a paper bag and a pair of tweezers. Carefully he lifted the glove up and dropped it inside the bag. "We'll have it tested for fingerprints at headquarters," he said.

Nancy heard the telephone ring and went to answer it. To her amazement the call was for her. It was from Mrs. Pauling, who asked if Nancy and her friends could come over to Bridgeford right away.

"You're needed here," she said. "It's a good thing you told John O'Brien where you were going and I could catch you."

"What's up?" Nancy asked.

"They're getting ready for a historical pageant to be held in connection with the formal opening soon," Mrs. Pauling told her. "I'm the chairman. I've just learned that the principals have been held up some place and can't get here in time for special pictures to be taken for a big magazine. The cameramen are waiting. How about you and your friends coming over and posing?"

"Why, certainly," said Nancy. "We'll be there as soon as possible."

She went to check with Mrs. Strook to be sure the elderly woman was all right. Mrs. Grover had arrived and said she would take good care of her friend.

When Nancy made her announcement to Bess, George, and the boys, they showed mingled feelings. Bess thought how romantic it would be. George objected to wearing "a flubby-dubby costume." The boys declared they would feel very silly. But all said that so long as Nancy had promised to do it, they would go.

Upon reaching Bridgeford, Nancy introduced the boys, then Mrs. Pauling took the group into a small white house where a governor of the state had once lived. The young people were given rooms in which to dress. As the six reappeared in their costumes, a few minutes later, all burst out laughing.

"I never knew I had such skinny legs until I put on these tight-fitting trousers," said Burt.

"And I should have curls hanging down under this bonnet," George remarked. "I must look like a lady convict of 1850 with my hair so short."

The merriment continued as the group went outside and walked over to the old stagecoach and horses, where two cameramen waited with John O'Brien. Introductions were made by Mrs. Pauling.

Ned, costumed as the driver, opened the door of the stagecoach for the girls to climb in. Nancy and Bess eagerly stepped up. Burt refused to follow and declared he was going to ride on top.

"I think I'll try that too," said George.

The others roared with laughter as the tomboyish girl tried to negotiate the climb in her long skirt. Finally, with the boys' help, she made it. Dave, who was to be messenger, pulled himself up to the front seat beside Ned.

"All ready?" the photographer called out.

"Let 'er roll!" Ned replied.

Cameras clicked for several pictures. Then the photographer called out, "Now I want to take some movies. O'Brien will pull the horses and stagecoach. Ned, act as if you were really driving, will you?"

The tow chain was attached and John O'Brien took his place at the wheel of the truck. A moment later the outfit began to move, but unfortunately the truck had started with a jerk. The stagecoach gave a sudden lurch, jostling George and Burt.

George lost her balance and toppled over the side!

Burt made a dive for her. He managed to seize George in time to keep her from falling to the ground. George, for her part, made a wild grab for the railing at the top of the coach and helped pull herself up.

The commotion had reached John O'Brien's ear and he had stopped short. George, shamefaced and a little disheveled, apologized. Suddenly she realized that the movie camera was still whirring. Turning to the photographer, she cried out:

"You didn't take my picture!"

"Of course. It looked very realistic," he replied, grinning.

"Well, don't you dare show it to anybody!" George snapped, but she knew from the big tantalizing smile he gave her that he would not accede to her request.

The balance of the photographing took place without incident. Mrs. Pauling thanked Nancy and her friends for all their trouble, then the young people said good-by and headed for Camp Merriweather.

The evening was spent catching up on home news, but by ten o'clock all declared they were weary from their day's experiences and said good night.

When Nancy reached her room, she sat down in a chair and gazed out the window, lost in thought. Her father had once told her that reviewing the various details of a case just before going to bed might bring a ready answer in the morning. Nancy often found herself instinctively doing this.

George lost her balance and toppled over the side!

Suddenly she jumped up and began to walk around the room as an idea came to her. She snapped her fingers and smiled.

"I wonder if I could possibly be right!" she thought excitedly.

CHAPTER XIX

A Midnight Attack

AT THAT moment the door between her room and the one George and Bess occupied suddenly opened. "Nancy, aren't you ever going to bed?" Bess demanded solicitously.

George followed. "Why, you're not even undressed!"

"Don't scold!" Nancy pleaded. "I just had an idea that I think may solve the mystery!"

As her friends watched, she dashed across the room to a bureau drawer where she had left the notes written by Great-uncle Abner Langstreet. Bringing them to the desk and turning on a bright light, she stared at the sides on which the signatures appeared.

"Some of these notes have penciled markings, you notice," she remarked.

"I see them," said George. "Just doodlings."

"Maybe not," Nancy murmured.

She creased one paper and laid it on top of another, so that the two drawings came together to form a horizontal staff and an arrow-shaped crosspiece at the center and to the right. Then she fitted a pointed section to the top. Finally, after creasing three papers into tiny squares, Nancy slid three circles over the center section.

"You're a genius!" Bess exclaimed. "That's a railroad semaphore!"

"It sure is," George agreed. "But what does it mean?"

Nancy smiled excitedly. "It's my guess that Mr. Langstreet buried his stagecoach along the railroad tracks near a semaphore."

"It's a marvelous deduction," said George. "But the question is, which semaphore. We might find ourselves digging in hundreds of places."

Before Nancy answered, she went back to the bureau drawer and this time pulled out the map Mrs. Strook had given her. After studying it carefully, she said:

"I'm convinced that Great-uncle Abner buried the old stagecoach on family property which runs along the railroad. Here's a strip and it isn't too many feet long. Even if we don't find the semaphore, we wouldn't have a great deal of digging to do at this spot."

Bess's eyes were wide open in astonishment. All sleepiness had gone out of them. "I think this is simply super, Nancy," she said in praise. "Right after breakfast tomorrow we'll all start out and go to this place."

"Oh, I can't wait that long," said the young sleuth. "It really isn't late. If we can get the boys to go, aren't you game to start digging tonight?"

"I'm game," said George, but reminded Nancy that she really had no right to dig on private property.

"That is a problem," the girl detective conceded. "I know what I'll do. I'll call up Art Warner and see what he says."

She hurried to the private phone booth on the first floor and called the lawyer. His wife, who answered, said he was working late at the town hall. "He's at a special meeting, but I know he'd be glad to talk to you," Mrs. Warner assured the girl.

Nancy put in a call and a few minutes later was talking to Art Warner. When she told him what she had in mind, he said he might be able to help her very easily.

"Please tell me exactly where that piece of property is," he requested.

After Nancy had described the location, the young lawyer asked her to hold the phone a few minutes. Returning, he said:

"I have good news for you. That property belongs to the town of Francisville. Taxes on it were not paid for a long time and the owner lost the piece. You have the permission of the councilmen to dig on it all you please."

"Terrific!" said Nancy excitedly. "I'll let you know the result. Any news for me about Mr. Langstreet?"

"I'm afraid not. But regarding any marriage of his, I think no news is good news."

Nancy said she must go now, and Art Warner wished her luck. She stepped from the booth and went to a house phone at the end of the registry desk. Calling Ned's room she asked him if he and the other boys would be willing to go out right away to do some sleuthing.

"Of course. But what's up?" he asked.

"I can't tell you now, but I'm sure I have a good clue this time."

Ned, who said he had not been asleep, would rouse Burt and Dave and they would all meet at Nancy's convertible in a few minutes. Nancy put down the phone, then went to speak to the night clerk. Smiling, she said, "I wonder if the lodge could do me a big favor? I'd like to borrow several garden digging tools—say six."

The clerk grinned at her. "More sleuthing, Miss Drew?" he asked.

"Now what makes you think such a thing instead of guessing that I might just want to transplant some flowers?" Nancy replied with a chuckle.

"When do you want the tools?" the clerk asked.

"Right away, if possible."

"I'll see that you get them. Where do you want the boy to take them?"

"To my car."

Nancy gave the license number, then said she was going to run back to her room but would return soon. When she and the other girls and the three boys met in the parking lot, the digging tools were standing up against the trunk compartment.

"You think of everything," Ned praised Nancy. "Where in the world did you get these?"

Nancy tossed her head. "From my friend the night clerk. And we'd better put them to good use because he'll certainly be asking what I accomplished."

Ned drove while Nancy, who was now very familiar with the general area, directed him to the special piece of property along the old railroad right of way. Presently she pointed out an overgrown, rutted lane where she thought he should turn down.

The narrow piece of property stretched a good distance from the road to where the tracks had once been. The railroad embankment was still there.

The group flashed their lights around and even beamed the headlights of the car on the surrounding area. If there had ever been a semaphore at the spot, it was gone now. The boys scuffed their feet along the ground and after a while Ned found part of a rusted iron pipe which stuck up alongside a stone.

"Nancy, do you think this might have been the pole that held the semaphore?" he asked.

"It might have," she replied. "Anyway, let's start our operations here."

For the second time within a few days, Nancy and her friends started digging for a buried stage-coach. The work went fast. The area all around the suspected semaphore pole was being spaded, pickaxed, and shoveled.

Presently Bess gave a squeal. "I've hit some-thing!" she cried out.

The others crowded around. Six inches below the surface they could see the corner of what ap-peared to be a rusted wrought-iron chest. Every-one helped to uncover the top of it.

"It *is* a chest!" Bess exclaimed gleefully. "Quick! Let's open it!"

There was no lock on the chest, but it took a little tugging to raise the lid.

"Bridles!" said Nancy excitedly. "One, two, three, four of them! The ones the stagecoach horses wore!"

There was nothing else inside the box, but Ned guessed that there must be other chests containing the various parts of the old stagecoach. Everyone worked feverishly. In a few minutes the top of

another chest of thin wrought iron was uncovered.
It held the box from under the driver's feet.

"Maybe the clue's inside the box," George
spoke up hopefully.

Burt flung back the ancient lid. There was
nothing inside.

Work went on for nearly two hours. By this
time twenty chests of various sizes had been
found. Each contained some part of the old stagecoach and all the pieces were in a fine state of
preservation.

"You were right, Nancy," Bess spoke up, "about
Great-uncle Abner Langstreet disposing of his
stagecoach with loving care. I suppose he made all
these chests in his blacksmith shop and drove over
here with them one at a time."

"That's all right," said George, "but where's
the clue he hid in one of them?"

"Don't be discouraged," said Nancy. "Accord-
ing to the notes, there are still ten chests to be
found."

The next one was unearthed by Nancy and Ned
together. Quickly Ned raised the lid. Inside was
one of the doors of the old stagecoach. And on top
of it lay an unaddressed envelope.

"The clue!" Ned shouted.

Nancy was so excited she was almost afraid to
pick up the envelope and look inside it. Her heart
was pounding furiously. She did take the envelope

out, however, but just then noticed a sweet, sickish odor in the air. Instinctively she held her breath as she turned up the flap of the envelope.

As Nancy started to look inside she suddenly noticed that her friends were acting very queerly. Bess and George seemed to fall to the ground in a faint. Burt and Dave staggered a few steps, then sank to the ground unconscious. Suddenly Nancy noticed Ned let the lid of the chest drop with a loud bang. He toppled over on the ground.

All this time Nancy had been holding her breath because she did not like the sickish odor. But now she knew she must fill her lungs with air.

As she did so, the young sleuth heard a noise a short distance ahead of her. Looking up, she caught a glimpse of Ross Monteith's face. Beside him was a shadowy figure, its arm stretched toward Nancy. On the wrist was a scar!

The hand reached for the envelope. At that moment Nancy blacked out and slumped to the ground.

CHAPTER XX

Honorary Citizen

IT was daylight by the time Nancy and her friends recovered consciousness. One by one they became fully aware of their surroundings.

"What happened to us?" Bess asked groggily.

"I think," said Nancy, "that our enemy put us to sleep with some sleeping gas he sprayed around."

"And the envelope!" George cried out. "Where is it?"

Nancy's listeners were stunned when she told them about Ross Monteith being there and the man with the scar on the back of his wrist having grabbed the envelope.

"The clue was in your grasp and they got it away!" Bess said woefully.

Ned arose and came to Nancy's side. "I feel mighty bad about this," he said. "I was just plain dumb not to think of our setting a guard. We laid ourselves wide open to an attack with all our lights turned on."

"Please don't blame yourself," Nancy said. By this time she felt that her mind was clicking almost normally again. "You know, it's just possible that those men did *not* get the clue after all."

"Whatever do you mean?" George asked.

Nancy reminded the others that there had been no name or anything else written on the envelope. "I admit I was getting pretty groggy at the time I was holding it, but the envelope didn't feel to me as though there was anything inside."

"You mean," said George, "that the real clue may be in one of the nine boxes we haven't uncovered yet?"

"That's right," Nancy answered. "But while we're looking, I think we should do what Ned suggested—set a guard. If there was nothing in that envelope we found, then those thieves will be back here to get the real one."

"More than that," said Ned, "I think the police should be notified. I'll drive to town and tell them while you continue the digging." He grinned. "And I'll bring you all some breakfast."

Nancy suggested that Ned also bring Art Warner, and told him where he could find the young lawyer.

The digging started again. Each chest was freed from the earth and quickly opened. The searchers looked for the elusive clue among the pieces of the stagecoach. Seven boxes had been opened and the eighth had just been raised when Ned Nickerson returned. With him were Art Warner, Sergeant Hurley, and Detective Takman.

"You're just in time to see the next to the last box opened," Nancy told them.

Everybody crowded around and Burt raised the lid. Inside the hand-wrought iron chest was the center seat of the old stagecoach. Nancy's quick eyes noted a small spot in the upholstery which looked as if it had been cut deliberately. Quickly she explored inside with her fingers.

"I feel something!" she cried out, and a moment later pulled an envelope from its hiding place. Smoothing it out, she read:

TO THE CITIZENS OF FRANCISVILLE

"This is the real clue!" she exulted. Then she turned to Art Warner. "As a resident of that town, will you please open this and see what's inside?"

As everyone stood around in awe, the young lawyer carefully opened the envelope with his penknife and pulled out a letter. As he read it aloud, looks of delight spread over the faces of his audience.

The letter was signed by Abner Langstreet and said that at the time the cornerstone of the town hall of Francisville was laid in the year 1851, Langstreet had been the person to put on the last bit of mortar to seal it. When no one was looking, he had slipped something inside the cornerstone box which he figured in years to come might be of great value to the town. He directed that when an emergency should arise, the cornerstone be opened and his gift used.

"How amazing!" Bess spoke up, as Art Warner stopped reading. "What's in the cornerstone?"

"The letter doesn't tell," the young lawyer replied. "But I should say that the time of emergency has arisen in Francisville. What do you all think?"

Everyone agreed with him and could hardly wait for the town fathers to open the cornerstone, so they might all see what the secret was.

"I'll arrange to have it done very soon, and we'll have a little celebration," Art Warner told the others.

George remarked, "And Mr. Langstreet's stagecoach belongs to the town too."

"Yes," said Nancy, then told the police officers and Art Warner that Mrs. Pauling had agreed to defray the expenses for having it fixed up.

Bess spoke up. "The old stagecoach should be put on display in Francisville—for a time at least, even if it's moved to Bridgeford later."

"What is to become of the stagecoach right now?" George asked. "We can't leave it here."

Art Warner had a suggestion. He said he had a radiotelephone in his car and would get in touch with John O'Brien. "I'll ask him to come and take these pieces to Mr. Jennings the carpenter."

Sergeant Hurley said that he and Detective Takman would stay there and guard the old stagecoach until John O'Brien arrived, then follow him to the carpenter's shop.

"And now let's have a celebration breakfast," said Ned. From the car he pulled out ham and egg sandwiches, thermos bottles of orange juice, and steaming cocoa.

When the orange juice was poured into paper cups, Ned raised his cup. "Here's to Nancy Drew, best girl detective in the world!"

"She's certainly amazing," Sergeant Hurley said.

Nancy thanked Ned for the toast, then said, smiling, "Sergeant Hurley, the whole story can't be told until you round up the suspects in the case."

"The captain was expecting some arrests at any moment when Takman and I left," the officer replied. "Why don't you ride into Francisville and stop at headquarters?"

"We'll do that," said Nancy.

The young people went directly there, while Art Warner said he would get in touch with the mayor and other officials to see about having the cornerstone opened very soon.

"Oh, I hope it will happen while I'm still at the lodge!" said Nancy.

The others waved good-by to the lawyer and walked into headquarters. Police Captain Dougherty was busy on the telephone. They waited for him to finish, then Nancy introduced herself and the rest of the group. She told him about the finding of the old stagecoach and the clue in it which might mean a great deal to the town of Francisville.

"You're just in time to hear some big news," he said. "My men are bringing in five prisoners. Mr. and Mrs. Monteith were finally located at a farm on the outskirts of the next town. Staying with them were the two thugs we've been trying to locate."

"And who's the fifth person?" Nancy asked.

"Judd Hillary. He'll have a lot of explaining to do."

The group arrived in a little while. Nancy and her friends were allowed to stay and listen to their confessions. Everyone of them glared darkly at the girl as if she had been personally responsible for their downfall. Ross Monteith's real name was found to be Frank Templer.

It was Judd Hillary who put the story together. He had a phobia against any changes in Francisville and the housing developments in particular, because his grandfather had told him valuable ore mines were under those very areas. Hillary had told this to the Monteiths and instantly Ross wanted to explore. It was his idea and Hillary's to try frightening people away.

The explosions had served a double purpose:

one was to scare people into moving, the other to open any veins of ore. The actual dynamiting job had been given to the two thugs who proved to be amateurs at it and had nearly caused fatal accidents.

"Did you send Nancy to the deserted farmhouse at the time of the second explosion, hoping she would be injured?" George asked Ross Monteith belligerently.

Audrey spoke up vindictively. "Of course not. He just wanted to keep her in one spot while he was busy with his friends getting the dynamite ready for the explosion. But I wish to goodness something *had* happened!"

"That will be enough," said the police captain sternly. "I will take your testimony later."

The officer went on to say that before the housing developments had been put up, every kind of test had been given to determine if there were any valuable mineral in that area. None had been found.

"I never heard that," Judd Hillary spoke up. "Why didn't somebody tell me?"

No one bothered to answer the man, but the captain said he had just had an FBI report on Ross Monteith, who used many aliases. Actually he was a confidence man who went with his wife to summer hotels looking for unwary victims.

"Monteith's work here was of a rather different kind, after he met Hillary and learned about the supposed ore," the officer added. "I daresay he had you hoodwinked, Hillary."

"I'll say he did, the skunk!" Judd Hillary burst out. "And he's the one who told me to get rid of Nancy Drew!"

"Let's hear your story, Monteith," the captain ordered.

The confidence man, beaten, said he had a Geiger counter in his cane and had been using it to try finding the valuable ore. "The only time it ever worked was right up at Camp Merriweather, but the clicking was caused by a big stone somebody rolled out of the garden into the woods there. It has traces of uranium in it, I think."

As the story of the Monteiths went on, Nancy and the others learned that the couple had overheard Nancy tell the other girls that Mrs. Strook had sent for her to solve a mystery. Ross and Audrey had followed them and eavesdropped. Hearing about the clue in the old stagecoach, they thought there might be a fortune hidden in it and were determined to obtain it before Nancy could. They were responsible for the hiring of the thugs, one an ex-seaman, to hijack Mrs. Pauling's stagecoach to search it, and to ransack the Strook home and tie up its owner.

Nancy asked if Ross had found anything in the envelope after using the sleeping gas. He admitted he had not. After a few more formalities, the prisoners were led away to be put in cells.

Bess gazed after them compassionately. "Oh, *why* can't people be honest?" she murmured.

As Nancy and her friends were leaving police headquarters, Art Warner walked in. "I have news for you," he said, smiling excitedly. "The cornerstone will be opened at four o'clock this afternoon. You'll be there of course. Do you think Mrs. Strook will be well enough to come?"

"I'm sure nothing could keep her away," Nancy replied. "We'll drive right to her house and tell her."

Before leaving, the young sleuth told about the capture of the Monteiths and the others, and gave him a sketchy account of their confessions.

"So all the mysteries are solved except what's in that cornerstone," Art Warner said. "Four o'clock can't come soon enough for me."

Nancy and her friends were very prompt for the ceremony. They had stopped for Mrs. Strook, who wore a very pretty pale-blue dress and matching hat. The Zuckers had been notified and were there to add their compliments.

Marjory whispered happily to Nancy, "My husband has secured a nice outdoor job with Camp Merriweather. They're going to build a new addition to the lodge."

"Oh, I'm so glad to hear that!" said Nancy.

At the edge of the crowd she could see John O'Brien and waved him to come forward. "You had a big hand in solving this mystery," she whispered to him, and he grinned. Mrs. Pauling, too, was present and congratulated Nancy warmly.

At last the mayor stepped forward. He gave the assembled audience a short resumé of Abner Langstreet's life, then read the letter.

"I wish he'd get busy and open that cornerstone," George whispered impatiently to Nancy and Bess.

Finally the moment for which they had been waiting arrived. A workman chipped out the masonry around the large stone on which were the words:

ERECTED A.D. 1851

After the use of a crowbar, and much tugging, he and two other workmen lifted the cornerstone out and set it on the ground. Behind it was a small metal box. The mayor pulled this out, and as a hush fell over the crowd, he raised the lid and took out an envelope.

"This says," he told the waiting group, " 'To Francisville from Abner Langstreet.' "

No one spoke as the mayor opened the envelope and put his hand inside. When it came out he was holding five blocks of four stamps each.

Mrs. Strook, standing close by, gave a gasp. "Why, these are Benjamin Franklin stamps of 1851 with the gum still on them! They're worth a fortune!" she exclaimed. "One stamp like these will bring $7,500. That would mean each block can be sold for at least thirty thousand dollars!"

A cry of astonishment went up from the crowd. Then Art Warner spoke up. "Why, they would bring enough money, when added to what Francisville can raise, to build a fine new school for our town!"

"That's right," the mayor agreed, and the other officials bobbed their heads. None of them could believe the town's good fortune.

There were tears in Mrs. Strook's eyes. "Bless my Great-uncle Abner!" she said. "There were times when I doubted his story. But Nancy Drew, here, never lost faith. All the credit for solving the mystery goes to her."

The town officials were loud in their praise of the young sleuth and her friends. As Nancy smiled she put an arm around Mrs. Strook. "This is the person who started the whole thing," she said. "She should have the credit."

The mayor said he agreed. "We must have a special celebration as soon as the old stagecoach is restored," he said. "Anybody have a suggestion as to what we might do?"

"I have!" John O'Brien spoke up, stepping forward. He told about how Nancy and her friends had dressed in costume and been photographed in the old stagecoach at Bridgeford. "I'd like to see them do the same thing here in Francisville, but make it part of a parade with real horses."

The crowd cheered and applauded, giving their approval to the idea. Nancy thanked everyone but said, "I think the passengers in the old stagecoach should be people who live in your town."

"No," said the mayor quickly. "You shall have the honor." Then he raised his hand over her head. "Nancy Drew, detective, is hereby proclaimed an honorary citizen of Francisville because of the fine work she has done for our town!"

The response was thunderous but Nancy hardly heard it. She was reflecting on how well everything had turned out for Francisville. For a brief moment she wondered whether her next mystery would be as much of a challenge. Although she had no way of knowing, *The Secret of the Fire Dragon* was to prove just as baffling and exciting.

When the applause had died down, Bess whispered, "You see, George, there *was* something to the clue in the old stagecoach. You lost your wager. Now you owe Nancy and me each a hand-knit sweater!"

George frowned, then said, "All right. This adventure was worth it!"